NEVER LET YOU GO

When Sofia Garcia's fiancé Jack says he needs space and then drops off the radar, she takes up her uncle's offer of a job as a tour guide in Spain, determined to move on with her life. But when she recognises a name on her latest guest list, she can't believe it's *her* Jack, who she hasn't heard from in eight months — he's come to Spain to try to win her back. Can Sofia find a way to trust him again, and is she prepared to risk her heart once more?

SARAH PURDUE

NEVER LET YOU GO

Complete and Unabridged

LINFORD
Leicester

First published in Great Britain in 2018

First Linford Edition
published 2019

A catalogue record for this book is available
from the British Library.

ISBN 978–1–4448–4261–6

Published by
F. A. Thorpe (Publishing)
Anstey, Leicestershire

Set by Words & Graphics Ltd.
Anstey, Leicestershire
Printed and bound in Great Britain by
T. J. International Ltd., Padstow, Cornwall

This book is printed on acid-free paper

Worst Fears . . .

Sofia stared at her clipboard. It couldn't be, could it? It had to be one of the commonest names in England. There was no reason to think it was 'her' Jack Brown. Not that he was 'hers' any more.

She smoothed down the list and forced herself to look up at the airport arrivals board. The plane had landed 20 minutes ago and the first few of her passengers would be arriving soon, having navigated passport control, customs and the game of cat and mouse that was luggage reclaim.

She took a deep breath and forced herself to smile. She was worrying over nothing and what she needed to do was focus on her job. That was why she had come to Spain in the first place.

Beside Sofia was the little stand that carried her uncle's holiday company logo and a sign which read 'Welcome to Spain!'

A few people started to appear through the electronic double doors, wheeling suitcases and looking travel weary.

The man leading the pack gazed at her but his eyes moved quickly to the holiday rep with the deep tan standing off to one side and he and his family trudged over to him.

Sofia returned her attention to the double doors as a dapper gentleman and his elegant wife emerged. The wife looked in her direction and Sofia smiled and waved.

'Welcome to Spain!' Sofia said, smiling at the gentleman who doffed his panama hat. She liked them both already which boded well for the next two weeks. 'My name is Sofia Garcia and I will be your tour guide for your holiday.'

'A pleasure to meet you, Miss Garcia. I am Tony Whitehead and this is my wife Greta.'

Sofia shook their proffered hands before ticking their names off of her list.

'Our coach and driver is waiting just outside. We have some more people to wait for but there is freshly squeezed orange juice, pastries and coffee on the coach. Please help yourself.'

Sofia pointed out the coach which could be seen just the other side of the exit doors, smiled one last time and then turned her attention back to the electronic doors as more people strolled through.

Twenty minutes later and Sofia had all but one of her passengers happily on board, making a dent in the box of fresh pastries she had picked up on the way to the airport.

She glanced back at the name of the last passenger on her list of neatly crossed off names. Jack Brown. It couldn't be, could it? She had no further details about her passengers except medical conditions, special requirements or food allergies and Jack Brown had none of the above, which wasn't all that comforting since that was true of the Jack Brown she was worried about.

Sofia shook her head and focused her eyes on the electronic doors that brought passengers through to the public arrivals area. Why would Jack come here, of all places? He was the one after all, who had said that he need some space.

To this day, nearly eight months later, Sofia had no idea what that meant. How could you want space from the person you said you loved — the person you said you wanted to spend the rest of your life with? But that was what he said he needed.

After the first couple of weeks, Sofia realised that when Jack said he wanted space what he actually meant was he didn't want to see her or talk to her and that was when she had been forced to accept her new reality. The life she had planned out with Jack so carefully was over and she needed to work out what she was going to do next.

The only thing that had appealed was

the offer from her uncle in Spain to come and be a tour guide for the season.

Sofia's dad was Spanish and so she had grown up with the language and the culture but had never spent any real time there apart from the occasional holiday and it had seemed like the perfect solution, giving her the time and space she needed to figure out what she wanted the rest of her life to look like.

Sofia had been in Spain for nearly three months and was loving her new job to the point that she was seriously considering working in the office for the winter and staying to guide for another season.

She had grown to love the friendly people, their relaxed attitude to life and the opportunity to really get to know the family on her father's side, who had always bemoaned the fact that they had had no time with their little Sofia. Here in Spain, she felt wanted and loved.

Not that her parents back in England didn't love of her — of course they did.

It was just that everything there reminded her of what she had lost and everything here seemed a million miles away and full of possibilities.

Sofia also loved the opportunity to show tourists the real Spain that she had grown to love. There were no mock Irish pubs on her tours. Instead there was history and culture and the beauty that Spain had to offer.

A man walked through the doors. He was dressed in a suit but from Sofia's experience that didn't necessarily exclude him from being one of her guests.

The laptop case was a little unusual but she had had a writer on her first tour who had said he never went anywhere without his computer since his handwriting was illegible, even to him.

Sofia smiled, just in case, but the man didn't even look at her as he walked towards a taxi driver who was holding up a printed sign which read 'Mr Williams' in bold black print.

Sofia was starting to wonder if she should phone the office to see if Mr

Brown had cancelled at the last minute or perhaps he had missed his flight from Gatwick? Sofia fished her mobile phone out of her bag and wedged it between her left ear and shoulder, as the phone was answered by Maria, her cousin.

'Maria,' Sofia said, 'I have one passenger who hasn't appeared and I wondered if he had phoned to cancel.' Sofia rattled off the words in Spanish and her improved accent made her smile. She suspected that most people would take her as having lived in Spain all her life.

'Hola, Sofia! No phone calls but I can call the airline and check to see if he was on the flight it you'd like?' Maria said and Sofia could hear the sound of manicured fingernails tap lightly on a keyboard.

'That would be great . . . ' Sofia started to say as the electronic double doors opened once more. A small knot of people, by the looks of their red hair all related, walked through, their thick northern accents marking them as being from Newcastle or thereabouts.

The group were not overly tall and in the background loomed a lanky figure, wearing sunglasses and wearing a black baseball hat, with the Barcelona football team logo on it. Sofia made a squeaking noise. Thousands of men and women had those baseball caps. Just because Jack had begged her to bring him back one from her last holiday to Spain didn't mean anything.

'You OK?' Maria's voice sounded in Sofia's ear and she had to force herself to speak.

'Fine,' she said, high pitched and in English. Maria tutted in a way that suggested she didn't believe her.

Sofia knew that she should say something soothing and reassuring but she couldn't take her eyes off the tall man who was separating from the Geordie family. She watched as he scanned the airport, looking for someone.

When his gaze settled on Sofia, he

removed his sunglasses, as if he were James Bond and she was a Bond girl and then Sofia knew. It was impossible but it was true. The Jack Brown on her guest list was the only Jack Brown in the world that she didn't want to see.

Painful Memories

'Hi, I believe you're looking for Jack Brown,' he said, holding out a hand to shake as if he had never seen Sofia before in his life.

Sofia glared at him and then spoke into her phone.

'No need to bother the airline, Maria, my last guest has just arrived.' Sofia said the word 'guest' as if it had a bad smell. She briefly closed her eyes knowing that she needed to make a decision in that instant. She could tell Jack to go away but if he had spent money to come and take the trip it seemed unlikely that he would give up that easily.

She had a coach full of guests who had not paid to see a soap opera acted out in front of them and so she knew what she had to do. Jack Brown was a guest, like any other, and she would treat him as such. If he could pretend that he had never met her, then so could she and that would be better for all of them.

'Mr Brown,' Sofia said and fixed a smile on her face as she shook the offered hand. She released the handshake as soon as she could. The sensation of her hand in his was full of painful memories. She crossed Jack's name off of her guest list.

'You are the last passenger to arrive with us today, so if you'd like to follow me we will make our way out to the coach.'

Sofia turned on the low heels that she always wore to the airport and walked towards the exit.

'Sorry about that,' Jack said.

Sofia blinked but didn't turn around. For a split second she wasn't sure what he was apologising for.

'My suitcase was the very last one off the plane. For a while I thought it might be wending its way to Italy or somewhere.'

'No problem,' Sofia said, flashing the briefest of smiles. 'The rest of the guests have been enjoying coffee and pastries on the coach so I don't suppose they have minded the wait.'

Tino was waiting for Sofia outside the coach and greeted her as an old friend. They had done many tours together and Sofia liked the older man, who talked often of his large family that he was extremely proud of.

'This is our last passenger,' Sofia said to him in Spanish. 'We can head off to the hotel.' Tino grinned and relieved Jack of his suitcase before stowing them in the luggage area under the coach.

'If you'd like to find a seat, Mr Brown,' Sofia said when Jack made no move to get on the coach.

'Ladies first,' Jack said and there was an all too familiar twinkle in his eye.

'That's very kind of you, Mr Brown, but I have some last minute details to go through with our driver. Please find yourself a seat and help yourself to coffee. We'll be on our way shortly.'

Sofia had nothing to say to Tino. They had their whole operation down to a smooth operation but she needed an excuse to get away from Jack and that seemed as good a one as she could come up with under the circumstances.

Jack grinned and climbed on board. Sofia could hear him introducing himself to each guest as he climbed on board, sounding like a famous person meeting fans.

Sofia cringed but when she did climb on board and take her seat at the front of the coach, the rest of the guests were smiling, clearly charmed by Jack's youth and exuberance.

Sofia felt all out of step with what she was supposed to be doing and so, as Tino joined the queue to leave the airport at Reus, Sofia shuffled the papers on her clipboard.

She had a full itinerary and a host of other information that she usually gave the guests on the journey to the first hotel of their stay. Sofia knew it all off by heart but somehow reading the words that she knew so well, had a calming effect.

Taking a deep breath she reached forward and picked up the microphone. She swivelled in her seat so that she was sitting half facing the back of the coach and opened her mouth to start her well prepared welcome speech.

Jack's face was grinning up at her from the seat immediately opposite her and no words came out.

All she could do was stare. It seemed like it was a nightmare and she expected to wake up any moment but no, even when she closed her eyes and reopened them he was still there. This was a nightmare but the waking kind.

Sofia knew that she was blushing and was also aware that her guests were looking at her expectantly. The few couples in the seats nearest to her started to shift in their seats and Sofia knew that she needed to get a grip. She plastered her best smile on to her face and looked up.

'Welcome to Spain!' she said with a

forced version of the jollity she normally felt at this point.

'On behalf of Garcia Real World Spain Tours, I would like to welcome you to the Costa Dorada. My name is Sofia Garcia and I will be your tour guide for the next two weeks.

'Over the next two weeks will be visiting the best that Spain has to offer. In the packs in the back of your seats you will find all sorts of information about our itinerary and the hotels we will be staying at.

'We are heading for the beautiful city of Tarragona, where we will arrive at our first hotel in about an hour, where lunch will be provided and there will be an opportunity for you to relax after your travels. For now, I suggest you sit back and relax and enjoy the country-side.'

Sofia shifted back in her seat so that she could see out of the large front windscreen. She could see that Tino was staring at her via the rear view mirror. She had thought she had spoken very fast, like a person desperate to get public speaking over and done with and now Tino had just confirmed it.

She tried out a smile and a small shrug but inside her head she told herself off. She was behaving like a schoolgirl whose crush had started to show her attention and it had to stop.

She had a job to do and there was no way that she was going to let Jack Brown distract her from that.

She still couldn't work out what his game was but in that moment, she made a decision. She didn't want to know and was going to do her best to avoid any possibility of finding out.

When the coach arrived outside the Hotel Cala Font, Sofia had too much to think about to worry about Jack. The hotel staff were very efficient and soon all the luggage had been transported to rooms and all of Sofia's guests were settled in the restaurant tucking into their lunch.

Through the glass doors, Sofia could

see that Jack was settled at a table with the Whiteheads and an elderly lady, Mrs Turner, who was travelling alone but seemed to have the independent travel spirit that Sofia loved to see.

Sofia could only see the back of Jack's head but it was clear he already had his audience enthralled as he regaled them with a story.

A thought occurred to Sofia that she quickly squashed down before she could get hysterical. Just because she had decided to act as though she had never met Jack before, didn't mean that Jack had, too.

What if he told the other guests about their relationship? What if he got them involved in whatever he was planning?

Sofia let out a groan which must have been loud since Inez on reception looked up with concern. Sofia smiled and tried to pretend as if nothing was wrong. Not easy, when she reminded herself that there were 13 more days of the tour ahead of her.

Unwelcome Invitation

When Sofia's tour group were all settled in the hotel bar with coffee or the drink of their choice she tapped her coffee cup to draw their attention. Thirty-two people looked towards her expectantly and Sofia focused on the 31 that she had never met before and who certainly had never had the opportunity to break her heart.

She could feel Jack's eyes following her every move and listening to every word but she made sure not to make eye contact, as she ran through the general itinerary.

'Your evening meal will be served between seven and half-past nine so please feel free to come when it suits you. The rest of this afternoon is free time for you to do as you please. Tomorrow we will start our first full day of touring with a walking tour of the

Roman ruins which make Tarragona famous.

'If I could ask you all to meet in the main reception for half-past nine tomorrow morning. The walking tour takes most of the morning and then you will have the afternoon and evening to explore Tarragona at your own pace. I will be working in the hotel office until five today so if you have any questions or concerns please do come and find me.'

She smiled around and was relieved to see her smile returned. It seemed none of her guests had found fault with anything yet. It didn't happen very often but occasionally one of her guests would be difficult to please and that was the kind of additional workload that she could do without, considering the man who broke her heart had decided, for reasons as yet unknown, to fly out to Spain and travel on her tour for two weeks.

Sofia watched them collect their belongings. Some headed out to the sun terrace and the others seemed set on returning to their rooms.

When they had all gone, Sofia headed to the office. It seemed that focusing on work might be just what she needed and she wanted to check the hotel bookings for the next week.

Sofia was staring at her laptop screen and trying not to think about the last time she saw Jack. It was a memory that she had worked hard to avoid over the last few months, knowing that it only brought her pain and didn't change anything, except to make her feel more miserable.

An email pinged in from Maria, checking that all the arrangements were in order, and Sofia expected her to start fishing for details on what had happened earlier. She put her fingers on the keyboard, wondering what she could say to put Maria off, without having to go into all the details. There would be time for that when the tour was over but it wasn't something she wanted to get pulled into right now.

There was a knock at the door and Sofia looked up, expecting it to be one of the hotel staff but then Jack's face appeared around the door.

'Mr Brown, what can I do for you?' Sofia said, barely glancing up from her keyboard in the hope of giving the impression that she was very busy and therefore had no time for small talk.

'Miss Garcia, I've just been speaking with the Whiteheads and the delightful Mrs Turner and we all agreed that we would like to invite you to have dinner with us this evening.'

Sofia paused in her typing.

'I'm sorry?' she said, knowing that she hadn't misheard, but hoping against hope that she had imagined what Jack had just said.

'The Whiteheads, Mrs Turner and I would like to invite you for dinner,' Jack repeated, acting as if he were oblivious to her stalling tactics, 'and we have all decided that we won't take no for an answer.'

Sofia raised an eyebrow. It was a

response she had used on Jack often when they had been together and she hoped it would have the desired effect. Jack's expression remained mild. Sofia sighed.

'I'm not sure I will have time for dinner this evening. I have a lot of work to do getting the tour ready.' Since that wasn't exactly the truth, Sofia crossed her fingers to ward off a white lie.

'I doubt Mrs Whitehead and Mrs Turner will accept that excuse. If I go back and tell them that, they are likely to get on the phone to your boss and complain that you are working too hard.'

Since Sofia hadn't really had the time to get to know either Mrs Whitehead or Mrs Turner she had no idea if the threat was real. The last thing she wanted was anyone phoning the office. Her boss, Uncle Alberto, would be quick to point out that all the organisation was done by the office staff and if Sofia had any problems all she had to do was pick up the phone.

She sighed and then pretended to look at the notepad beside the laptop as if it had a long list of jobs on it. There was nothing for it, she was going to have to go to dinner with Jack and only hope that he behaved himself.

'Fine,' she said, in a manner that suggested she had been put in an impossible situation and she wasn't happy about it.

'Brilliant!' Jack said with a beaming grin, 'We've agreed to meet for a drink in the bar at seven o'clock sharp.'

Sofia opened her mouth to say that she couldn't possibly make drinks first but Jack had disappeared before she had the chance and there was no way she was going to run after him.

As much as she didn't want to speak to him, she wondered if she should leave him some kind of note asking him to refrain from discussion of any past relationship.

She sat back in her chair and stared out of the window which looked out on to the long drive of the hotel. She shook her head. If she broached the subject, maybe that would make it worse. Maybe he would take that as an encouragement, that she was interested and open to discussing the past.

Sofia pushed her chair away from the desk and stalked over to the tiny fridge which held bottles of water and helped herself.

What she couldn't figure out was why he was here. Why now, after all this time? All this time she had spent working hard to put that chapter of her life behind her and trying to heal her heart. He had no right to just turn up, after eight months of nothing, and demand anything from her.

What she needed was a plan — a plan that considered all possible outcomes from the evening's dinner. She walked back to the desk and picked up a pen and paper and wrote down some headings: 'He brings up the past', 'He indicates that we may know each other', 'He pretends we have only just met'.

Somehow having the stark reality of

the situation written down in front of her in her own words made it feel a hundred times worse. She wasn't sure that she was ready to deal with any of those situations. Even the thought of pretending that they had never met before that day was not something that she really wanted to contemplate.

Why did Jack have to turn up now, just when she felt like her life was getting back on track?

Sofia glanced at her watch. Half an hour until they were supposed to be meeting for drinks. If she wanted to have a quick shower and get changed then she needed to get a move on.

Getting to Know You

With her hair wrapped in a towel, Sofia looked at the contents of her suitcase, which mostly consisted of her tour guide uniform clothes which she wore during the day, so her choice was limited.

She had one maxi dress, a pair of shorts and her scruffy floppy trousers that she usually just wore in her hotel room to be comfortable at the end of a long day. Sofia was fairly sure that the hotel would frown upon her wearing shorts to dinner, so that just left her maxi dress.

She pulled it on and looked at herself with a critical eye. It was made of the kind of fabric that survived being scrunched up in a suitcase for two weeks. It was black with a small pattern in white and she knew it suited her, showing off her curves and her light tan.

It was one of her favourite outfits but there was a problem. Her reflection was telling her that she looked as though she had made an effort and she wasn't sure that was the message that she wanted to give out to Jack.

Sofia's eyes drifted back to the case, wishing that she had brought more outfits with her — not that she had any reason to think she would need them.

She walked into the bathroom and dried her hair, deciding against make-up, and pushing her feet into her one pair of flat sandals.

The piece of paper, with her supposed plan, lay on her bed and it didn't have much written on it. Despite staring at her problem for several hours she still didn't have a firm idea of what she should do and that was mainly due to the fact that she still had no idea why Jack was here.

A small part of her heart, one that she thought she had successfully smothered over the months since she had last seen him, was determined to believe he was there to win her back. And that was probably the crux of this dilemma. She wasn't sure that she wanted him back.

No, perhaps that was entirely truthful — she wasn't sure that she could risk the heartache of trying again. It had taken her so long to recover that she couldn't shake the idea that the past was best left in the past.

A glance at her watch told her that she was procrastinating and making the others wait for her. Sofia hated to be late and in fact had her watch set ten minutes fast, but despite that, today she was late and even that didn't seem to be enough to convince her legs to carry her out of her room and down the stairs.

The watch was a thin woven silver band with a small face and it had been a present from Jack. It had been the only reminder of him that she had allowed herself to bring to Spain and she had told herself it was because she loved the watch. But now she wasn't so sure.

Without giving herself time to argue, she slipped the watch off of her wrist and placed it in her small floral bag. With one last deep breath, knowing she couldn't put it off any longer, she opened her room door and headed towards the stairs.

As predicted, the Whiteheads, Mrs Turner and Jack were waiting for her in the bar. They had found a table near the French windows that overlooked the hotel's pool area and seemed deep in conversation, which Sofia hoped meant they weren't annoyed that she was late.

She took a moment to remind herself that the most important thing was the guests. This was her job, after all, and one that she had come to love. She vowed not to let Jack's presence get in the way.

'Hello, everyone,' Sofia said with a well-practised smile. 'I hope that you are all happy with your rooms and the hotel.'

The group turned to look at her and

Sofia was greeted with warm smiles.

'Everything is wonderful, dear,' Mrs Turner said, patting the seat next to her, 'but we didn't invite you to share dinner with us so that you could work. We all agreed you probably could do with an evening off.'

Mr and Mrs Whitehead nodded and Jack grinned up at her as she took the seat that was offered.

'I'm here to make this the best holiday I can for you all.'

'Well, it's been wonderful so far so there is no need to worry. Now enough about work, we were just finding out a little bit about each other.'

Sofia risked a glance in Jack's direction at that final comment but he just continued to smile and Sofia couldn't tell whether he had shared information about their past relationship or not.

'Perhaps we should go around and introduce ourselves again,' Mrs Whitehead said, smiling kindly at Sofia, 'so that we don't put Sofia at a disadvantage.'

Sofia smiled back at her with gratitude.

'Good idea. Shall I begin — or do you want to?' Mr Whitehead said, beaming at his wife.

'Tony and I are retired,' Mrs Whitehead said without directly answering her husband's question but they seemed so in sync that it felt unnecessary.

Sofia realised that they were holding hands across the table and watched Mrs Whitehead give her husband's hand a squeeze.

That was what she missed most, she thought, the closeness to another person, where words weren't always necessary. She suddenly realised the table had gone quiet and that all eyes were focused on her.

'My turn?' Sofia asked somewhat unnecessarily but needing to say something to give herself a few moments to compose her answer. The others looked on expectantly.

'Well, my dad is Spanish. He met my mum and moved to England. I have an older brother and a younger sister. Garcia Tours is owned by my dad's brother, Uncle Alberto. When he asked me to come and be a tour guide for a season I thought it would be a great opportunity to spend more time with my Spanish family and also introduce people to the Spain that I know and love.'

Sofia's speech sounded carefully prepared, which it was. A lot of her guests were curious about their tour guide's background.

'How marvellous!' Mrs Turner said. 'We will expect you to know lots of things about the places we are visiting, since you are a local.' Sofia smiled at the twinkle in the older lady's eyes.

'I'll do my best,' Sofia said, smiling. 'And what about you, Mrs Turner?' Sofia saw a little of the light go from Mrs Turner's eyes.

'Please call me Barbs. My name is really Barbara but only my mother ever called me that. Harry said he didn't think it suited me.'

Sofia nodded, thinking she probably

understood now why there was an air of wistful sadness about her.

'We made all these plans, you see . . . to travel when we retired, but it wasn't to be.' Barbs seemed to swallow with effort and then managed a smile. 'But I promised Harry that I would do all the things we had planned to do so here I am. This trip was on my list,' she added to Sofia with a wink.

Sofia wasn't sure what to say. She thought she had known heartache when things had ended with Jack but to lose a partner was so much worse and made Sofia feel a little guilty that she was making so much of having Jack on the trip.

She looked up and realised that Jack was studying her closely. There was nothing else for it, she thought, time to take the bull by the horns, as the Spanish liked to say.

'And what about you, Mr Brown?'

'Please call me Jack.'

'Of course,' Sofia said. 'So, Jack, what about you?'

'I had a friend at university who used to wax lyrical about this part of Spain. She loved it here and so when I had some leave to take from work without any fixed plans, I thought, why not?'

Sofia nodded slowly. She was the friend, of course. She and Jack had met at university on their second day and had been inseparable for the rest of their time there. She wasn't sure if the others had thought it was odd that the friend wasn't named.

'Is there anything you particularly want to see?' Sofia asked, feeling as though she needed to steer the conversation on to safer ground.

'Monserrat,' Jack said. 'I'm told it's a real highlight.

Sofia nodded again. It was one of her favourite places. She loved the history and the mountains and she had often spoken about her first visit when she was a small child.

'Many of my guests are keen to go there,' Sofia said, not knowing what else to say and not wanting to admit that it was one of her favourite places on earth, in case the others started to put the pieces of the puzzle together.

'I'm looking forward to the Roman ruins,' Tony said. 'I've become a bit of an amateur archaeologist in my retirement. I always want to do it but there was never a right time.'

'Till now,' Greta said with a smile. 'Now Tony goes away on digs over the summer.'

'Well, you will have a guided tour tomorrow and then the rest of the day to go back and look at them in detail,' Sofia said. 'I have several books on the history of Tarragona if you'd like to read them.'

Sofia watched as Tony's eyes lit up and Greta rolled her eyes, but with real affection.

'You need to be careful, Sofia, or Tony will be taking over the tour.'

'I always appreciate opportunities to learn new information for future tours,' Sofia said with a smile.

No Chance of Romance

Sofia felt herself relax. It seemed clear that whatever Jack's reasons for being here, and she doubted it was simply because she had done such a good job at university of telling him how wonderful it was, he had no plans to share it with the other guests.

The Whiteheads and Barbs Turner were great company and had a whole array of exciting travel stories to share. Sofia could see why Jack had been drawn to the little group.

The food was delicious, as always, and the wine flowed freely, although Sofia was careful only to have one glass. She needed to be on top form for a full day of tour guiding the following day.

After their early start and a day of travelling it was clear that the group were in need of an early night and so they broke up soon after coffee was served.

Sofia was tired herself. The sight of Jack and all the associated emotions meant that she was ready for bed, too.

Everyone said goodnight and headed off to the lifts. The Whiteheads and Barbs got off on the first floor, which left Sofia alone with Jack.

She wasn't worried. She knew that Jack's room was on the third floor and so it would only be a matter of seconds before he left the lift as well.

The lift chimed and the doors opened on to the third floor but Jack made no move to get out. Sofia looked at him but he was busy gazing up at the ceiling.

'Jack, this is the third floor,' Sofia said, trying to keep her voice even. She was too tired for games and just wanted this day to be over.

'I know,' he said with a grin.

The doors started to close again and Sofia reached out to press the button that would hold the doors open.

'Your room is on this floor,' Sofia said, using her most patient voice that she had developed after the one or two difficult guests she had had to deal with in her time as a tour guide.

'It was,' Jack said cheerfully, 'but I asked if I could move up to the fourth floor so I could have a better view.'

Sofia narrowed her eyes. Her room was on the fourth floor. She had no idea what game he was playing but it had to stop now.

'The view is no different,' she said, her voice making it clear that she was not charmed by his actions.

'Oh, I disagree.' He flashed Sofia his best smile. She could feel the corners of her mouth twitch but forced her lips into a disapproving straight line. She raised an eyebrow, too, just in case he didn't get the message. It seemed to have the right effect as his smiled faltered a little and he crossed his arms — a defensive gesture that Sofia knew well.

'OK, you got me,' he said, before holding both hands out in front of him.

A thought occurred to Sofia. She had

read about it in a magazine but surely not — not Jack.

'Are you stalking me?' she blurted out. Her words were loud in the small space and Jack took a step back and bumped into the lift wall.

'What? No, of course not!'

Sofia's mind started to go through what she could remember from the article. He had certainly turned up in a place she wasn't expecting.

Now it was her turn to cross her arms and she eyed him suspiciously. Surely he couldn't be after some form of revenge. It was Jack who had ended it, not the other way around. Her face creased with a frown as she tried once again to work out what was going on.

'Whoa, Sofia, hold on. It's nothing like that! I can see your mind is going to some dark place.'

Sofia kept her expression the same, even though part of her wanted to smile, feeling like she was seeing the real Jack, her Jack, for the first time since he had arrived. She shook her head, as if she wanted to shake some sense into herself.

She had heard nothing from him for eight months. That time had been incredibly painful and she was just now putting her life back together. She wasn't about to let him step back in and offer two weeks of a sort of holiday romance before he took off again and left her alone once more.

'I missed you,' Jack started to say but by now Sofia had convinced herself that she wasn't going to fall for his charm. She couldn't afford to. She didn't think her heart could take going through that all over again.

'Soph. I wanted to see you again, to talk to you.'

Sofia shook her head.

'It's been over eight months. Jack. You could have just sent a text. You have my number. There was no need to fly all this way and spend all this money. I'm sure you could say whatever you need to in an e-mail or something.'

As they were both walking down the

hotel corridor Sofia glanced at the door numbers and noticed that she had been so lost in thought that she had walked past her room so she stopped.

'I could, but it didn't seem right after all the time that has passed.' Jack reached out and Sofia felt his hand brush hers but she pulled away.

She couldn't allow herself to get sucked back in, not for two weeks. They might be two wonderful weeks but what would happen at the end? Jack would go home and she probably wouldn't hear from him for another eight months and she just couldn't risk it.

She couldn't fall apart again. She didn't know if she would have the strength to put herself back together.

'You shouldn't have come,' she blurted out as she turned on her heels and fled for her room. She fumbled in her purse for the plastic card that would give her entry into her sanctuary, all the while aware that Jack was gazing at her. The door lock beeped and Sofia shoved it open before disappearing inside. She leaned against the door and closed her eyes.

'I wanted to talk to you, too, but you ignored all my attempts,' she said softly to the room as a few warm tears started to roll down her cheeks.

Sofia allowed herself five minutes — a technique that she had developed to cope in those early days. She was allowed five minutes of wallowing and then she had to do something else, anything else, to occupy her mind and move on.

Sofia checked her e-mails and read through the schedule for the next day, even though she knew it off by heart.

She unpacked her wash things and placed them in the bathroom before getting into her pyjamas. The paperback that she was currently reading was lying on the bed and she picked it up, intending to read a bit before bed.

After she had read the first line at least ten times, with no idea what it actually said, she put it back on the bedside table.

Her mind was going over and over the last conversation, playing it back like a movie.

Had she been unfair to Jack? Should she have at least listened to what he had to say? Maybe he had been hurt as much by it all as she had.

She turned over in bed as all too familiar feelings of pain and hurt were joined by a new sensation, guilt. She pulled a pillow over her head, as if that might block out the unwanted thoughts and tried to sleep.

Best Case Scenario

By five o'clock in the morning, Sofia knew she was wasting her time. Even if she did fall asleep now, she would only feel worse when her alarm clock went off and so there was nothing else for it. She needed to get up. She slid her legs over the side of the bed and rubbed at her eyes.

A picture formed in her head of Jack sleeping soundly and it did nothing for her mood. After a quick shower, she threw on her tour guide uniform and went in search of coffee. The bar and breakfast area wouldn't be open yet but the reception was open 24 hours and they usually had a pot of coffee on the go.

One glance at the mirrored walls in the grand reception area told Sofia that she probably should have taken the time to put on some makeup. Her face stared back at her, pale beneath her tan and with bags under her eyes that she could probably have used to go shopping.

'Hola,' a soft voice said from behind the reception desk. Sofia smiled and asked if there was any coffee. The night receptionist was not someone she knew terribly well but she was greeted with a smile and a hand pointing in direction of the office, from which the smell of coffee wafted.

With a coffee mug in her hand Sofia felt more ready to think about how she was going to handle the day.

Seeing Jack again was probably going to be more awkward than their first meeting at the airport but there wasn't much she could do about it.

For a few seconds she had considered throwing him off the tour but couldn't imagine how she would justify that to her uncle without first explaining exactly who Jack was.

Alberto was a fiercely protective man, and guarded his family like an angry bear. He would completely understand Sofia's actions, she knew he would, but he would also probably feel the need to come and give Jack a piece of his mind — not something Sofia thought she could face, either.

No, there was nothing else for it, she was going to have to act as if their conversation last night had never happened. Perhaps Jack would be happy to go back to pretending they had never met.

Fortified by coffee, Sofia nipped upstairs and did her best to cover up the fact that she hadn't slept a wink. Once she was satisfied that she was looking as good as was humanly possible, she headed down to breakfast.

She liked to greet all her guests first thing in the morning, to check that all was well, so that they could head off on the day's activities without delay once breakfast was over.

There were a few earlier risers and so Sofia nipped into the restaurant to greet them before returning to her post by the door.

'Morning, ladies. How did you sleep?' Sofia asked with a smile to a group who were travelling together.

'Wonderfully, thank you. The hotel is marvellous,' the lady at the head of the group said. The rest smiled and nodded and so Sofia took that as a good sign.

Having counted all the guests into breakfast, Sofia knew that they were all there — all but one. Jack had never been a morning person but part of Sofia hoped that perhaps he had changed his mind and was going to head home.

She thought she might be able to get a partial refund for him. It wasn't her fault that he had been foolish enough to come all this way without checking with her first but she didn't like the thought that he would be so out of pocket.

She was just considering ringing the office to see how to go about it when the lift chimed to announce the arrival of another guest.

The hotel had over 100 rooms and so it was entirely possibly that it was someone unconnected with her group but somehow she knew without looking that it was Jack.

'Good morning, Sofia,' Jack said with a smile as he breezed past her and into the dining-room.

She watched him go, her mouth slightly open in surprise, as he sat down at the table with the Whiteheads and Mrs Turner, who had clearly saved him a seat.

Sofia turned away, all thoughts of eating breakfast herself gone. She felt a coldness in the pit of her stomach. She knew she was being ridiculous. This had been the best-case scenario, that Jack would pretend they had never met before, but why then did she feel like she was being rejected all over again?

She made her way quickly to the small office that the hotel made available to her, with her fingernails digging in to her palm, a trick she used to keep her emotions at bay. With the office door closed behind her, she let out a gulping sob.

Sofia was lost in thought and had

tears running down her cheeks when her phone beeped. It was an alarm that she set herself to make sure she had time to get everything they needed on to the coach.

This morning they didn't need the coach, as everything they were going to see was in walking distance from the hotel. What she needed to do was stop feeling sorry for herself and get on with her job, she told herself firmly.

She pulled a small compact mirror from her bag and looked at her reflection.

'You can't go getting upset at every little thing.' Sofia spoke the words softly. There was no-one else around to hear them but still it would be embarrassing if anyone did. 'This was what you considered to be the best-case scenario,' she told herself. 'You can get through two weeks of pretending to be strangers.'

She said these words louder, feeling the need to convince her reflection which looked sad and a little bedraggled. Thankfully, she had gone for waterproof mascara and so her makeup only needed a little touch up, rather than a complete redo.

Sofia shook herself. Now she was stalling and if she wasn't careful she was going to be late and that would only raise suspicions that she didn't want raised.

She reached for the rucksack she always took on walking tours. It contained spare bottles of water, suntan lotion and a range of other 'in case of emergency' supplies.

She reached for the pile of tourist maps on her desks, took a deep breath and then headed back to reception.

A quick head count told her that all of her group were present and she smiled at them.

'Good morning, everyone, and welcome to the walking tour of Tarragona. This morning we will visit the local Roman sights and also take in the mediaeval cathedral. Now Tarragona is a busy place and so I will have this so that you can follow me in a crowd.'

Sofia produced a small flag which

was decorated with the Garcia Tours logo. It clipped on to the back of her rucksack and her group smiled and nodded.

'I also have some maps for each of you so you can explore this afternoon in your own time.' Sofia handed them out one by one, ensuring her gaze was focused on the maps rather than the person she was handing them to.

She knew that Jack was there within the group but wasn't quite ready to look at him just yet.

'We will stop for coffee or a cold drink and you'll be pleased to hear that the pastries at this particular coffee shop are excellent.'

Holding Back the Tears

It took only ten minutes at a slow pace to reach the first set of Roman ruins that Tarragona was proud to display. Sofia spent around 10 minutes explaining the history of the site and what it was used for before leading the group inside.

'The fort was built by two brothers who felt the need for protection from the Carthaginians,' Sofia said, as she led them up the long slow slope and in through a gap in the wall. 'This was an important part of the Western Roman Republic and the emperor Augustus once wintered here in Tarragona during one of his campaigns.

'The best way to tour the site is to follow the audio tour which will be waiting for you in the small shop.' Sofia started to hand out small paper tokens. 'Please hand these to the shop assistant and you will be given an audio tour in English. Take your time and I will be waiting here at the exit for you so we can go on to our next site.'

Once the tokens were handed out, the group joined the short queue and then each member appeared with a set of headphones and a small electronic box. A few waved and smiled at her but most seemed to be concentrating on what the electronic guide was telling them.

Sofia let out a sigh of relief. She had survived the first hurdle and she had managed to avoid eye contact with Jack. For his part, he seemed happy to immerse himself in the tour.

'I was wondering if you would be interested in touring with me.' Jack's voice sounded at her right elbow, making her jump just a little.

Sofia groaned inwardly.

'I think you will find the audio guide more informed than me,' Sofia said, forcing her face to hide any emotion she was feeling.

It also wasn't true. Sofia had read many books on the history of the town but the owners of the site preferred tour groups to take the audio tour, saying that large groups moving around interfered with the enjoyment of others.

'Somehow I doubt that,' Jack said and for the first time since he had arrived, his usual grin was missing.

'Unfortunately, guided tours are not permitted inside the walls,' Sofia said, glad for once that such a rule was in place.

'I can't see how they could object to two people walking around. We could even put in our earphones and pretend we were listening.'

Sofia knew that Jack was studying her closely but she couldn't bring herself to look at him. Her defences were so weak that one look at his smile might make the tears come again and she didn't think that would be good for either of them.

'Come on, Soph. I won't bite and I promise I won't ask anything other than about this amazing site.'

Sofia looked now and saw that h was smiling a little. Sofia sighed. This was not what she wanted but could she resist that smile?

'Fine. But I intend to keep you to your word,' Sofia said in her most serious voice.

'Of course, you know me, I'm all about the history.'

Sofia could have laughed then, since the opposite was true about Jack, but she didn't want to encourage him. She also knew Jack well enough to know that she could either stand here and argue with him or give him the guided tour, since he was not one to give up when he had his mind set on something.

'Fine, but it will have to be quick,' Sofia said, holding out a hand and indicating that Jack should take the lead.

Jack had a triumphant look on his face and Sofia started to wonder if this had been his plan all along. Since she was the tour guide she would be forced to be polite and it would be difficult to refuse him, when his request, on the surface, appeared reasonable.

She followed him through the shop and on to the start of the numbered tour that ensured visitors all went in the same direction. She reminded herself that whatever happened she was not going to discuss the past or, for that matter, the future.

'So what can you tell me about the Roman brothers who built this place?' Jack asked.

Sofia raised an eyebrow. He had been listening to her, which in itself was a surprise.

'We don't know too much about them. They were both statesmen and officers in the Roman legion. They built the defensive walls that we will see later on the tour. They fortified the town and built this fortress. This was an important site for the Romans.

'The land around here is good for growing crops and the port meant that it had a constant supply of goods coming in and going out.'

As Sofia started to speak she realised the best way forward was for her to keep talking. If she talked then it would be difficult for Jack to speak, let alone slip in any difficult questions.

She opened her mouth to speak again when she saw Barbs Turner fighting against the natural flow of the other visitors and for once she wasn't smiling. She looked positively worried, the colour having drained from her face.

'Oh Sofia, I'm so glad I've found you,' Barbs said, her voice trembling with worry. 'It's Tony — he's had a bad fall.'

Sofia tried to swallow but her mouth had gone dry. This was the worst aspect of being a tour guide, when someone was injured or fell ill on a tour. It was a part of her job which she never felt completely prepared for.

She was a born worrier, she knew that and she also knew that was not helpful in these kinds of situations.

'Why don't you take me to him.'
Jack's voice cut through Sofia's panic. 'I
can help.' Jack sounded so calm and in
control that it eased Sofia's panic just a
little.

'Of course you can! You're a paramedic!' Barbs sounded relieved. 'Oh,
I'm so glad you're on the trip!'

Jack smiled and held out an arm,
indicating that Barbs should lead the
way. As he fell into a quick step behind
her, he glanced over his shoulder at
Sofia who couldn't seem to get her legs
to move.

'It's OK, Soph,' he said softly, 'I can
look after this.' Then he turned his head
and disappeared through the crowd.

Sofia was nodding in agreement and
then remembered her responsibilities
and why she was here. It was great that
Jack could offer assistance but that
didn't mean it was right just to leave
him to it and so she weaved through the
crowd, following the top of Jack's head
that she could just about make out.

When they arrived at the scene,

Greta looked remarkably calm, kneeling beside her husband and whispering reassurance. Tony was propped up against a Roman wall, his expression a mixture of pain and embarrassment.

'It's my own stupid fault,' Tony said, directing his words to Jack. 'I wanted to get a better look at the architecture and so I broke the rules and climbed the steps, missed my footing and turned my ankle. I expect it's just a sprain.'

'All right if I take a look?' Jack asked. When Tony nodded, Jack made short, careful work of removing Tony's right shoe and sock.

Sofia and Barbs both gasped at the sight. Tony's ankle had swollen and was turning a dusky colour.

'Can you wiggle your toes?' Jack asked.

Tony did his best, wincing in pain and Sofia wasn't sure she had detected any movement. She didn't know enough about things medical to know whether that was a good sign or a bad one. Jack was gently probing Tony's foot with careful fingers.

'I don't think it's broken but we'll need an x-ray to be sure,' Jack said before turning to Sofia. 'Tony won't be able to put any weight on this and so can you see if they have a wheelchair we can use?'

Sofia nodded and hurried back off the way she had come. A quick conversation in Spanish and she had let the staff know that one of her guests had taken a tumble. A wheelchair was quickly offered and an ambulance was called.

Sofia wasn't sure whether that was what Jack had intended but the concerned staff had insisted and Sofia didn't think it was her place to argue.

Instead, she took the wheelchair and made her way back to Jack and Tony. It wasn't easy negotiating the chair around the people and over the uneven surface but she made it back.

'Right, Tony, now what I want you to do is let me take your weight while you stand up using your left leg. Your right foot won't take your weight right now and so I'm going to ask Sofia to hold it gently so it doesn't get banged around.'

Jack threw Tony's arms around his shoulder and braced.

'On the count of three,' he said as Sofia leaned over and gently lifted Tony's ankle off the ground. She was rewarded by a smiling wince and did her best to be as careful as she could, as with Jack's help, they manoeuvred Tony into the wheelchair.

Sofia walked ahead and Jack followed her, pushing the wheelchair around the small groups of people, some of whom took the time to stand and stare.

By the time they reached the small entrance shop, Sofia could see the ambulance pulling up on the road outside. The two paramedics walked up to greet them. Sofia quickly explained what had happened in Spanish and then translated as one of the paramedics repeated the examination of Tony's ankle, asking questions and looking to Sofia for the Spanish reply.

As Tony was loaded into the ambulance Sofia knew she had a dilemma.

She didn't want to leave Tony and Greta alone at a hospital where they didn't speak the language. It was likely that there would be some staff that spoke English but still, she didn't like the idea of them going alone.

'I'll go with them,' Jack said as he held out a hand to Greta as she climbed in the back. 'Let me have your mobile number and I'll keep you updated.'

Sofia opened her mouth to argue but Jack was still talking.

'You need to stay with your other guests and I'm sure between the three of us we can navigate the Spanish healthcare system.'

Tony and Greta both seemed to be watching her carefully and so Sofia smiled. She didn't want to be the one to give the game away.

'That would be great, Jack, thank you.'

'Mobile?' Jack asked.

Sofia gave him her number and he tapped it into his phone. When he was half way through it was clear that he realised that Sofia's number hadn't changed. He glanced up and their eyes locked.

Sofia knew that Jack still had her number in his phone. For eight months he had been able to contact her and he hadn't.

Jack was the first to look away and Sofia closed her eyes briefly as she tried to block out the memories that threatened to overwhelm her.

When she opened them again, Jack was walking with the paramedics as they wheeled Tony down to the waiting ambulance.

Listen to Your Heart

Sofia had explained to the rest of the group what had happened and reassured them that Tony was fine and would, no doubt, be rejoining the tour soon.

The whole group had agreed that it was lucky that Jack had been with them and that he was a paramedic. For the first time since his arrival, Sofia found herself agreeing with them.

The rest of the group had continued their tour and then Sofia had left them to their own explorations of the beautiful city. She had returned to the hotel and, after having updated the office of recent events, found herself waiting for Jack to call and it was an all too familiar and all too painful experience.

This time she knew she couldn't blame him. No doubt Spanish hospitals were as strict as UK ones over the use of mobile phones and probably he didn't want to leave Tony and Greta to step outside and call her.

Still, it didn't make it any easier as memories of the long months after his shock announcement filled her mind. She thought she would wear out her phone, checking for messages or texts every five minutes. Her phone and the lack of any contact from Jack had dominated her life for far too long. She put her phone down and tried to focus on the plans for the following day.

When her phone did ring it made Sofia nearly jump out of her skin and she glared at it. No name came up. She had taken the decision to remove Jack's details from her phone when she had left the UK for Spain. It had seemed like an important step in her broken heart recovery.

Of course, what it couldn't do was erase his phone number from her memory so when the number appeared on her screen she knew it was him.

'Sofia, hi, it's Jack.'

Sofia smiled to herself. Jack seemed to think that she had removed his number, too.

'Hello, Jack. How's Tony?'

'Tony is fine. He told me to tell you that he is sorry for messing up the tour.'

Sofia could hear muffled voices in the background.

'Please tell him not to be silly and that I'm sorry he tripped.' Sofia smiled. Tony and Greta were on track to be some of her favourite guests.

'Tony's ankle isn't broken, it's just a bad sprain.'

'What a relief,' Sofia said and felt some of the tension leave her.

'Unfortunately, he is going to need to be on crutches for a while so I've arranged to hire some, as well as a wheelchair. Tony isn't keen on the wheelchair idea but I suspect there will some places on our tour that he might need a rest from hopping everywhere.'

'That's great, thank you,' Sofia said. She hadn't even thought that far ahead but Jack was right, of course.

'We are just waiting for a prescription for some pain relief.'

Now Sofia could hear Tony in the background, firmly saying that he didn't need them and then Greta's soft voice telling him not to be silly. Just hearing them talking as they always did made Sofia feel that perhaps today wasn't turning out to be the disaster that she thought.

'I'll sort out a taxi for you,' Sofia said, making a note on the pad she kept by her computer.

'No need, already done. I'll text you when we're near the hotel.'

'Thanks, Jack,' Sofia said, feeling a little that he was doing her job for her. She might not be a paramedic but she was an expert at organising things. She felt immediately ashamed at her reaction. Jack was doing all the right things, for today at least, and to be anything other than grateful was churlish of her.

'I'll see to everything here and arrange for some lunch for you all,' she said.

'Great, we'll see you soon.'

With that, Jack ended the call, leaving Sofia feeling even more confused about her feelings. She was grateful, of course, that Jack had been there to help out. She was sure she would have muddled through but injuries and illnesses were not her thing and if she were honest she probably would have panicked a lot more if she had been on her own.

But she didn't particularly want to be glad that he was here in Spain. It complicated her life and brought up too many unwelcome feelings that she had spent months trying to erase. Sofia shook herself. There would be time to think about this later, when she was alone. What she needed to do now was go in search of the hotel manager to arrange for lunch to be ready.

When her phone beeped the next time, Sofia was ready for it. She checked the message and then made her way outside to wait for the taxi. Five minutes later, she and Jack were helping Tony out of the car. He refused the offer of the wheelchair insisting that he was perfectly capable of using crutches.

Sofia walked Tony and Greta to the restaurant where a special table had been laid for them. Once they were settled she realised that Jack hadn't followed and so went to look for him. She found him by the lift doors, looking as if he was going up to his room rather than having some lunch.

'Jack?' she called as the lift doors opened. He turned and waved but stepped into the lift and so Sofia hurried to follow him. Once she was inside, he pressed the button for his floor and the lift started to move.

'I'd arranged lunch for you. Aren't you hungry?' Sofia asked, wondering what was going on.

'I know, but I thought you probably hadn't eaten and might want to eat, too,' Jack said, avoiding eye contact with her, which was unusual to say the least.

'Why would that stop you having lunch?' Sofia asked, feeling confused.

'Tony and Greta guessed,' Jack said,

sounding guilty as he looked down at his feet.

'Guessed about us?' Sofia asked but she didn't really need to, she already knew. They both walked into the lift as the door opened. It seemed a good a place as any to continue their conversation without the risk of being overheard.

'They asked me and I didn't feel I could lie so I said that we had met before. Then they sort of nodded at each other as if it confirmed something they already suspected.' He looked up. 'I didn't tell them anything else, I promise.'

Sofia sighed. At least it was Tony and Greta who had guessed. She had the feeling that they were not the kind of couple to go around gossiping and she suspected they would keep the revelation to themselves.

'That's OK. I guess it was sort of inevitable.'

'I didn't come here to make your life difficult,' Jack said and now he did look up and Sofia could see from his face that he meant what he was saying.

There was an obvious question on Sofia's lips. The problem was she wasn't sure she was ready for the answer but then if she didn't ask it, the rest of the tour would continue to be stressful and awkward as her mind filled in those blanks with all sorts of made up stories. She took a deep breath and let it out just as the lift pinged to say they had arrived at Jack's floor.

'Why did you come?' Sofia's voice was so soft she wasn't even sure that Jack would be able to hear her.

'Because I'm an idiot,' Jack said as he stepped out of the lift.

Sofia was too stunned to react, to even process what he meant by that. The last image she had of him before the lift doors closed, was him walking along the corridor with his hands in his pockets and his head bowed.

Sofia leaned against the side of the lift and closed her eyes. What did he mean? Did he mean that he shouldn't have come? Or that he should have come but should have handled things differently?

But, worst of all, her heart seemed to have settled on one further possibility — that he was an idiot to have ever let her go.

Sofia put her hand to her chest as she felt as though her heart was about to leap out of it and needed to be restrained.

The joy and excitement that the thought brought was quickly squashed by the sensible part of her brain, that reminded her of all the pain and hurt she had suffered and the promise that she had made herself.

She had promised not to risk her heart again, at least not on Jack. And all that raised an even more important question: what was she going to do now?

Unanswered Questions

The lift had been recalled to the ground floor and since Sofia hadn't pressed any buttons, that was where she was taken. When the doors opened, she walked out in a daze and headed for the restaurant.

The truth was, she had no idea what Jack had meant and right now she didn't have the time or the emotional energy to want to find out. So instead she focused on work, the thing that had got her through the months of heartache.

She walked into the restaurant and pulled up a chair beside Greta and Tony.

'How are you feeling?' Sofia asked sympathetically.

'Like a fool, an old fool — but otherwise I'm fine. Please don't worry.'

Greta handed Sofia a basket of bread

and not knowing what else to do, Sofia helped herself. She didn't feel hungry at all but if she was going to join guests for lunch she couldn't really just sit there and not eat. Tony handed her the dish containing the small packets of butter and then the plate of ham.

Lunch passed very pleasantly with Tony and Greta regaling her with stories of their seven grandchildren and there was no mention of Jack, for which Sofia was very grateful.

'Will you be OK getting back to your room?' Sofia asked as their coffees were cleared away. 'I can get the wheelchair out of the office for you.'

'I think we'll leave the chariot until I really need it, but thank you,' Tony said with a smile. Greta helped him to his feet and Sofia watched as they made their way to the lift and then disappeared.

Sofia had already rung the office to ask if the Whiteheads could change to a ground-floor room if possible.

Tony might not be happy to be

pushed around in a wheelchair but at least a ground-floor room would mean they wouldn't have to bother with the lift.

Sofia's mobile phone rang and she recognised the office number and so headed in the direction of her small office to take the call.

'Hola, Maria,' Sofia said.

'I hope you've got time now,' Maria said in her no nonsense tone, 'Because I'm expecting a full explanation.'

Sofia frowned.

'What do you mean?'

The noise Maria made down the phone made it clear that she wasn't going to fobbed off that easily. Sofia sighed but said nothing, still hoping that Maria might not have connected all the dots.

'Mr Brown is your Mr Brown, isn't he?' she said triumphantly.

Sofia sat down. This was going to be a long conversation.

'That's why you were so freaked out at the airport, wasn't it? I can't believe I didn't put two and two together!'

Sofia said nothing. There didn't seem to be anything to say.

'Well? Are you OK?' Maria demanded.

'I'm fine,' Sofia said, wondering if that was true. She had been through every emotion in the last 24 hours and now she wasn't sure whether she was OK or not.

'Oh, Sofia. Why didn't you tell me?'

'I was hoping that I wouldn't need to.'

'You must talk about these things,' Maria said in the Spanish way that brooked no argument. 'It is the only way that you will feel better.'

'I feel like I've talked about it enough,' Sofia said.

Maria had been curious as to why Sofia had suddenly agreed to join the company as a tour guide and unlike her father, Uncle Alberto, Maria was not one to buy into Sofia's explanation that she needed a change of scene without asking why.

'No, not now. Now is different. Why

is he here?' Maria said swapping into English as she did sometimes with Sofia.

'I don't really know,' Sofia said, wondering if she should just march upstairs and ask him.

'You not know?' Maria's English got worse if she was excited or exasperated and Sofia couldn't actually tell which was the case now.

'You ask him?'

'Sort of.'

'What is this 'sort of'?

'He said he came because he's an idiot.'

'He needed to come all this way and spend all his money to tell you what everyone else knows?'

'I don't know what he meant by that, Maria. I don't know whether he meant that he was an idiot for coming all this way or whether he was an idiot for breaking up with me.'

'Clearly he is both,' Maria insisted.

Sofia smiled. Her cousin was fiercely protective of her and when Sofia had finally shared her story, Maria had been enraged by the way Sofia had been treated.

'Perhaps . . . but I still don't really know why he's here. He's gone back to pretending that we've never met before now — although two of the guests have guessed that we know each other from home.'

Maria snorted.

'You should go ask him, right now. He has no right to play these games.'

'I think I might have encouraged him to pretend that we'd never met.'

'It is still his fault. He did not tell you he was coming! The tour is on a free time break, yes?'

'Yes,' Sofia squeaked, knowing what was coming next.

'Then you go find him and confront him!' Maria said.

Sofia winced. Whilst she was half Spanish on her father's side, she had grown up in England and it just didn't seem like the done thing — not to mention the fact that the idea of doing it made her knees feel wobbly.

'I can't!'

'Of course you can!' Maria said in the tone of voice that suggested there were no earthly reasons not to. 'Or I will phone him.'

Sofia's eyes went wide. She could not let that happen. She loved Maria but she didn't think Jack being roundly told off by a person he had never met would help the situation at all.

'No, no. No need for that. I'll go and speak to him.'

'Good — and soon as you have finished you will call me back, yes?'

'Yes,' Sofia said feeling like a little girl who had been told to go and apologise to a grouchy neighbour for kicking a ball over their fence.

'Well, why are you still on the phone to me? Go, go!'

'Bye, Maria,' Sofia said and couldn't help smiling. Maria had been a big help in sorting through her emotions and working out what she wanted to do with her life.

Her cousin had been understanding

and kind but with the kind of no-nonsense approach that Sofia had needed after months of weeping.

So perhaps she was right now? Sofia would probably feel better if she got to the bottom of things, then at least she wouldn't be walking on eggshells for the next two weeks.

Sofia walked to the lift and bumped into the group of ladies who were on her tour. They were laden down with shopping bags and Sofia smiled.

'Ladies! It looks like you've had a good time.'

'Excellent shopping,' one of the ladies agreed. 'How is Mr Whitehead? We were so worried about him.'

'Wonderful that we had our very own paramedic with us to assist him,' another lady said and Sofia wondered if she was being studied closely for her reaction or just being a little paranoid.

'Mr Whitehead is fine. He has a badly sprained ankle and will need to use crutches but he is back at the hotel and tells me he is ready to continue the tour tomorrow.' Sofia smiled, hoping that they could move the conversation on from Jack.

'Oh, that's wonderful news,' the lady said. 'Will you be joining us in the lift?' she asked as the lift door opened.

'No, thank you.' Sofia tried not to look too relieved at having an opportunity to escape any further Jack-related conversation. 'I have some work I need to be getting on with. I'll see you at dinner.'

Sofia knew that Maria would not be put off for long and would most likely follow through on her threat if Sofia didn't go and speak to Jack.

Her eyes wandered to the stairs which were through a fire door, which made it seem unlikely that any other guests would be using them.

Sofia pushed through the door and started to walk upstairs. She made it to the second floor before she realised that someone else was coming down.

Time to Talk

Sofia paused. This was not exactly how she had imagined this conversation starting but perhaps the stairs weren't such a bad location. It seemed unlikely they would be disturbed or spotted together.

Since Jack was heading down the stairs there didn't seem to be any point in her walking up any more and so she stayed where she was and waited.

She could hear Jack's footsteps on the stairs, echoing loudly in the empty staircase and she was also fairly sure he was talking to himself although she couldn't make out the words.

Sofia stood still facing that dilemma of how best not to make a person jump. Should she stand still and be quiet or should she make noise to let him know she was there? She was pretty sure that whatever she did, Jack would be more than a little surprised to see her there.

Before she could make up her mind, Jack was standing halfway down the staircase frozen in place. His cheeks coloured and Sofia could guess that whatever he was talking to himself about had something to do with her.

She tried to hide her smile. She hated to admit it but it kind of felt good that the boot was on the other foot for once.

'Hello, Jack,' she said, the situation making her feel braver than she had before. She watched as he tried to smooth the look of shock and surprise from his face and morph it into his usual grin.

Sofia wasn't fooled, though — there was nothing he could do about the bright red cheeks which were acting like a beacon of his embarrassment.

'Soph. I wasn't expecting to meet you here,' Jack said with slightly forced jollity.

Sofia wanted to point out that he must now know how she felt but she thought he had probably suffered enough embarrassment for one day.

'Me neither, but I was actually looking for you.'

'For me?' Jack said and Sofia could tell he was stalling for time. Now she couldn't help smiling and looked down at her feet to try to hide it.

'Yes, I wanted to talk to you,' she told the floor.

'Did you?' Jack sounded both surprised and hopeful and Sofia wasn't sure how that made her feel. 'I wanted to talk to you, too.'

Sofia nodded. Now she was here she wasn't sure how to go about asking what she wanted to know.

'Do you want to go first?' Jack asked into the silence that seemed to have formed between them.

Sofia shook her head. Maybe if Jack went first he would answer her burning question without her needing to have to voice it.

'OK,' Jack said and sat down on the bottom step of the flight of stairs from the third floor. Sofia followed suit and sat on the top step. She clasped her hands in her lap and tried to calm down her heart which was beating as if she had run up the stairs.

'I wanted to apologise to you for just turning up,' Jack said. Sofia swallowed the lump that had suddenly appeared in her throat. Not trusting herself to speak, she simply nodded. 'And for not contacting you — at all.'

Sofia returned to a close inspection of her shoes. She knew if she looked up now she would most likely cry.

'After I said what I did, I wasn't sure what to say.'

Sofia frowned at her feet. The excuse sounded weak to her ears and she could only imagine what Maria's response was going to be. But the thought made her feel bolder.

'Why did you say it?' Sofia asked, her memory replaying that last conversation they had had eight months ago, which had seemed to come out of the blue, making it all so much more painful.

'I was feeling like I was a little trapped.'

Sofia looked up sharply, anger pushing out the desire to cry at the painful memories of the time after.

'Trapped?' she said, one eyebrow raised, wondering if this was going to be a much shorter conversation than she had thought.

Jack shifted uncomfortably on the step.

'That was the wrong word. It's really hard to explain.'

Sofia looked at him expectantly. He was going to have to try and she wasn't going to help him. She was too angry and hurt in that moment to risk trying to put any of her current thoughts into actual words. Jack was looking around the staircase as if he was in need of inspiration.

'It was stupid . . . ' he started to say and Sofia agreed with him. He had always been so good at finding the right thing to say but that ability seemed to have deserted him completely now. Jack shook his head as if trying to shake his thoughts into some sort of order. 'I regretted it the moment I said it.'

Sofia felt hope flare but pushed it down. It wasn't difficult, as she reminded herself of the pain she had suffered as a result.

'I just felt like the rest of my life was planned out and I panicked.' He looked at Sofia, his gaze direct and almost pleading for her to understand.

'I thought that was what you wanted,' Sofia said. 'Most of the plans we came up with were yours.'

'I thought it was, too,' he replied softly.

Sofia felt the familiar blanket of pain settling over her. Jack was here to try to explain his actions — not because he wanted things to be different.

Perhaps with time, an explanation for those actions, which were so unexpected at the time, would help but right now Sofia felt as if time had been reversed and she was back on the late summer day where her life had unravelled before her eyes.

Sofia stood up suddenly. She was sure that she was going to cry and she didn't want to do that in front of Jack, not again.

What she needed to do was escape to her room where she could try and figure out all that had just happened and perhaps ring Maria for some sympathy. What she didn't want was to be in Jack's company a moment longer.

She risked at look in his direction and he looked confused.

'I understand.' She wasn't sure she did really but it was the only thing she could think to say to bring this conversation to an end. 'What I don't really understand is why you came all this way but maybe you felt you needed to explain face to face. A letter would have done.' Sofia stopped talking as she felt the tears threaten to choke her.

'Sofia . . . '

She cut him off.

'You've said what you came to say and I appreciate it.' She forced the words out. 'So, you can go home now if you want or you can stay on the tour. I don't mind.'

That was a lie, she did mind but she still felt a stab of guilt that he had spent so much money. It wasn't her fault, of course. It had been entirely his own decision.

'But I would appreciate, if you do decide to stay, that you don't discuss our personal history with anyone on the tour.'

She turned away from him, sure that she wouldn't be able to keep it together for a moment longer and fled down the stairs and out of the nearest door. Jack stayed where he was on the stairs, his head bowed, staring at his hands that were clenched together in his lap.

'That wasn't what I came to say,' he said the words out loud to the empty staircase. 'I came to say that was the worst mistake of my life. I came to beg you to take me back and tell you that you are the love of my love.'

Jack's placed his head in his hands as he tried to work out how his plan had gone so terribly wrong.

Above him the door to the third floor

closed so quietly he didn't notice. Barbs Turner, feeling a little guilty at over-hearing a conversation that was not meant for her, allowed the door to click into place, but knowing exactly what she needed to do.

Calling a Truce

By the time Sofia was changing for dinner, she was feeling a little better. She had been on the phone with Maria for over an hour and Maria had given her some good advice.

At least now Sofia knew, Maria had pointed out, that her decision to come to Spain and start a new life was the right one and what she needed to do was focus on that.

Maria had been sure that Jack would turn tail and run back to England and had also been certain that there was no way he was getting his money back, not after the way he had treated Sofia.

The tour would be heading to Barcelona at the end of the trip, where the main office was based, and Maria would be waiting for her in the apartment that they shared.

Sofia looked at herself in the mirror.

She had cried herself out and felt that she might be ready to face him again, not to mention the rest of her guests.

She needed to pretend that nothing had happened and when Jack was gone, either today or at the end of two weeks, she could go back to focusing on her new life here in Spain.

She walked out of her room and down the corridor to wait for the lift. It was empty when she stepped in but on the way down she picked up the Whiteheads and Barbs Turner.

'Tony, how are you feeling?' Sofia asked.

'Still like an old fool, my dear, but I think the swelling is going down.'

Greta gave him a look which suggested she thought the opposite was probably true but it was a look that contained such affection that Sofia felt some of the emotion bubble up inside her again. She forced herself to take a slow deep breath and smile. Barbs was looking at her closely and so she didn't want to give anything away.

'So, the tour tomorrow?' Barbs asked and Sofia felt grateful for the distraction.

'Well, we're going to tour some of the Roman features that aren't within walking distance so we will be doing that by coach.' Sofia turned to look at Tony. 'We'll take the wheelchair but there shouldn't be too much walking.'

'Ah, yes,' Tony said, balancing his elbows on his crutches and rubbing his hands together. 'The Roman aqueduct. One of the most impressive in this part of Europe, I'm told.'

Sofia followed the group out of the lift and across the wide reception area as Tony continued to explain the amazing feat of engineering that had produced the aqueduct which was, according to Tony, way ahead of its time.

Sofia smiled and nodded. She knew much of what Tony was saying but it was lovely to listen to someone who was so enthusiastic about a subject that Sofia loved. Most of the other tour guests had taken their seats and so Sofia excused herself and made her way around to each table, checking that all was well and asking about their afternoon in Tarragona.

The starter was served whilst Sofia was doing this and her gaze turned to the table where Jack had taken to sitting. The Whiteheads and Barbs Turner were there but the other two chairs were empty.

A quick scan of the dining-room told Sofia that Jack was absent. She wasn't sure if she felt relieved or a little sad but it would certainly make dinner easier than she expected.

As she took her seat next to Barbs, Sofia wondered if Jack had packed his bags and left. She wasn't completely surprised that he hadn't informed her. The last conversation had been awkward at best and she suspected painful for him, too.

Even though he was the architect of his own pain, she still felt for him, just a little. She would need to check with reception to see if he had checked out of his room. Sofia felt sure that Maria would have sent her a text if Jack had cancelled his place directly with the office.

'Sofia, well, I imagine you have had quite a day,' Barbs said, smiling up at her. Sofia nodded and forced her mind to focus on the here and now.

'All part of being a tour guide, and believe me, I have had more eventful days.' Not that a guest hurting himself and then being rescued by her ex-boyfriend wasn't up there with the best of them, she thought to herself, but had no intention of sharing that thought with her guests.

'Oh?' Barbs said. 'Well, now you'll have to tell us!'

And so, dinner continued with Sofia talking about tours she had taken and some of the people she had met and she didn't notice when Barbs and Greta threw in the odd personal question about her life.

It was only when dinner was over that Sofia realised that none of them had asked where Jack was. Perhaps Jack had spoken to them and told them of his plans?

Not that she could ask. That would be very suspicious behaviour, the tour guide not knowing where one of her guests was and the last thing she wanted was more people to jump to conclusions about her and Jack.

After dinner they invited Sofia for a drink but she made her excuses, saying that she had a few things to prepare for tomorrow. In any case, was in need of an early night after the events of the day.

The Whiteheads and Barbs seemed to accept this. Sofia did one last round of checking in with the other guests and reminding them all of the time the tour would leave in the morning and then she headed to reception.

The receptionist was a young man whom Sofia didn't know, something she was grateful for as she asked him to check whether Mr Jack Brown had checked out.

'No, madam. Mr Jack Brown is still a guest and is due to leave us the day after tomorrow,' the young man said in Spanish. Sofia thanked him and then headed back to the lift.

So Jack hadn't left, he had just decided not to have dinner with them, which again made her wonder if he had spoken to the Whiteheads. She wondered what excuse he had made to avoid her.

Part of her was grateful. A little more time before having to see him again was a good thing but another part of her was annoyed. He was the one who had come here, come here to tell her the reasons for calling time on their relationship. He was the one who, if anything, had made her feel worse about the whole thing and now he was hiding away from her. If he was going to behave like that then surely he should just go home?

The lift doors opened and Sofia stepped in without looking, just as the person inside stepped out. They collided quite heavily and Sofia wobbled and would have fallen if arms hadn't reached out for her.

'Oh, I'm sorry, I wasn't watching . . . ' The voice trailed off and Sofia didn't need to see him to know who it was.

'Sorry,' he said again and Sofia made herself look up at him.

'I wasn't looking, either,' she said, aware that behind her some of the guests were walking towards the lift.

Sofia and Jack stood and stared at each other for a heartbeat before both becoming aware that the guests waiting for the lift were looking at them curiously. Jack was the first to come to his senses and he stepped out of the lift, making Sofia step to one side, too.

'You didn't come to dinner,' Sofia said, hoping to sound like a concerned tour guide rather than an ex-girlfriend who had secretly hoped Jack would decide to leave the tour and go home. It seemed to do the trick as the group of guests stepped into the lift and disappeared from sight.

'I wasn't feeling hungry,' Jack said, his eyes looking anywhere other than at Sofia.

'Oh,' Sofia said, 'so where are you going now?'

Jack froze as if he had been caught out.

'I was going to go out and . . . get some fresh air.'

Sofia had known Jack for too long to be fooled.

'You're going out to get something to eat, aren't you?'

Jack winced and then nodded looking at the floor.

'I didn't want to make things awkward.'

'What like turning up on a tour run by your ex?' Sofia asked but she was smiling. Somehow the ridiculousness of the situation had cut through everything else and she couldn't help but see the funny side to it.

Jack looked at her now and he was looking fairly sheepish.

'Look,' Sofia said, 'you've paid for

99

your holiday and it is going to be impossible for us to try to avoid each other for the rest of the two weeks so why don't we agree here and now that we will carry on as we did at the start?'

Jack looked surprised and Sofia had to admit that she had surprised herself with her words but she was pleased that she had been able to say them, to behave and sound like a grown-up despite the hurt that she felt.

And somehow saying those words seemed to lessen the hurt. Surely behaving like grown-ups would make the next two weeks easier?

'That sounds good,' Jack said softly. 'I don't deserve it but I'd like that if you think you can manage it.'

'Of course,' Sofia said as she felt a pang of affection for him. For the man that she had thought she would one day marry. 'Well, I'll let you get some food but please don't feel like you need to avoid the meals in the hotels in the future.' Sofia managed one more smile before she stepped purposefully into the lift where she didn't have to work quite so hard on her composure.

A Nudge in the Right Direction

Sofia had managed to get some sleep and as a result felt almost human the next day. The good thing about days that were difficult is that once they were over you had the sense that you wouldn't have to deal with anything quite so bad for some time. She had survived and was feeling pretty good about that fact. It was a testament to how far she had come, she decided, since that dreadful day when Jack had shattered her world.

Sofia was the first to arrive at the dining-room. She had already been to the office and checked in with Tino to confirm departure times and their planned tour for the day.

Sofia was feeling back in control and it felt good. She now felt that she could get through the next two weeks, and maybe even enjoy it as she usually did and then Jack would go home and she could focus on her new life in Spain, putting the pain and heartache finally behind her.

Sofia welcomed each guest in turn and then headed into the dining-room, determined to find a seat other than with Jack. As her eyes scanned the room she realised that some of the guests had changed from the initial seating and that all the other tables were now full, save one.

She was now faced with a choice. She had either to sit by herself or take a seat at the table with the Whiteheads, Barbs and, of course, Jack.

She knew that sitting by herself was be the equivalent of writing a sign in the sky that she didn't particularly want to sit with Jack and so she had no choice.

As she took her seat opposite Jack she couldn't keep a frown from her face. This surely had to be his doing. Jack shifted in his seat and wouldn't look her in the eye which made Sofia's frown deepen.

If this was due to some sort of strange plan on his part she had expected him to look at her and challenge her to comment but instead he looked as uncomfortable as she did.

'Sofia! Lovely for you to join us,' Tony said in the kind of voice that suggested he had no part in whatever plan was afoot and was in fact completely oblivious to any discomfort on her part.

'Good morning, everyone. Thank you for saving me a seat.' Sofia knew that she shouldn't say anything but she couldn't help herself.

'Oh, you're welcome, Sofia,' Barbs said with a smile and a twinkle in her eye. Sofia saw that Jack was staring at Barbs, too, and it made her wonder.

Had Jack told Barbs about their past? He might have. Not since their conversation the night before, maybe, but perhaps he had said something prior to that.

'So, Jack, you were telling us before about your life as a paramedic. It sounds terribly exciting. I always thought you'd have to be particularly brave to face the unexpected every day.'

Barbs directed her comment to Jack, who flushed and shoved a croissant into his mouth to give himself a few moments to compose himself. Sofia raised an eyebrow at him when he looked in her direction, as if to say, go on then. Jack swallowed with effort.

'Most of it is fairly mundane, to be honest, Mrs T. But on occasion it can be a bit hair-raising or downright crazy.' Jack managed to smile but Sofia could see he wasn't his usual self.

Of course, it served him right if he had spilled the beans to Barbs. He had no right to share personal information like that. If he was expecting any sympathy or help for that matter from Sofia, then he could think again.

'I'd be interested in some of the crazy things that have happened,' Tony said, joining in but once again appearing oblivious to the awkwardness of Jack's reply.

Greta looked at her husband and gave a little shake of her head, before catching Sofia's eye and giving her a knowing look. Sofia was being to feel like the situation was well beyond her control. Did Greta know, too? Had Jack told all of them? It really was just too much!

Sofia felt Jack's eyes flash in her direction but she was too cross to try to decipher any hidden messages. It seemed like everyone was now in on their secret and that meant that however they both chose to behave it was going to be awkward. Sofia made a show of looking at her watch.

'Well, I'll leave you to finish your breakfast. I need to go and check on Tino and the coach,' Sofia said, making her voice sound loud and cheerful. She needed to do no such thing but didn't think she could sit there in the strange atmosphere.

She had heard a lot of Jack's stories

before but now it felt too uncomfortably like the two ladies at the table were trying to set her up on some kind of blind date, encouraging him to show off in an attempt to impress her. Sofia smiled and then stood up.

'Well, my dear, I must say I think you work terribly hard.'

'I enjoy it, Barbs, so I've no complaints. We're planning to leave at nine-thirty so I will see you soon.' And with that she headed out of the dining-room and to the safety of her office.

Tino was ready to go, as Sophia knew he would be, but in order to distract herself from the situation with Jack, she went through and double checked that she had all the relevant guides to hand out.

'Sofia?' Tino said and she looked up from her checking of the cardboard boxes that she stored all the maps and guides.

Tino's face looked concerned and Sofia had a horrible feeling that Maria might have spilled the beans. She forced her face into a smile and waited for him to speak.

'You are OK?' he asked in English. Sofia kept the smile in place but decided she was going to have to have words with Maria later.

She knew that she was trying to help but this was really not helpful. Tino was a typical Spanish man which meant he would no doubt feel the need to be fiercely over-protective and that could only make the situation far worse.

'I'm fine, Tino. How are you?' Sofia asked in Spanish and hoped that her point would be made.

'Fine,' he said, eyeing her suspiciously and Sofia had to suppress a sigh. Now she would have to keep an eye on Tino too, in case he decided that Jack needed a good talking to. The noise of the automatic hotel doors sliding open was a welcome distraction and Sofia turned and started to welcome her guests on to the coach.

Jack was the last to arrive. The only

empty seats were right at the front of the coach behind Tino, and directly opposite Sofia's seat. She had no choice but to sit there since the microphone only reached so far.

Sofia sat down and picked up the microphone and started to explain to her tour guests what the day would hold.

'Our first stop is the Roman aqueduct, one of the finest examples in this part of Europe. It has largely been untouched through the unsettled history of this region. It will take us around thirty minutes to reach the site and so until then, sit back, relax and enjoy the sights.'

Sofia put the microphone down and risked a look in Jack's direction. He was facing away from her, staring out of the window but Sofia had the impression that his eyes weren't seeing anything. He looked miserable and she felt a pang of guilt.

As much as she wished that he would simply go home so they could put this whole mess behind them, she didn't think she could bear to see him look so low for another ten days.

She twisted in her seat to get a good view of the coach and all her guests seemed to be happily engaged in conversation or looking out of the windows. She risked one more glance and then shuffled across the aisle so that she was sitting next to Jack.

Jack turned to her, looking surprised, but it could do nothing to mask the sadness around his eyes.

'Are you OK?' Sofia asked, suddenly finding that she didn't know what to say.

'I'm fine,' he said and made an effort to smile at her. Sofia knew him too well to be convinced by it. Despite the hurt both recent and from months ago, Sofia's heart contracted. You couldn't love someone as deeply as she had loved Jack and not be affected when he was in such obvious pain.

'I believe you, thousands wouldn't,' Sofia said. It was an expression they used to use all the time and she was pleased to see Jack's smile become more convincing.

'Really, I'm fine, Sofia.'

Sofia chuckled softly.

'Of course you are. That's why you look like someone has died.' Sofia's hand went to her mouth as she realised what she had said. Her eyes went wide at the thought that perhaps that was the reason Jack was sad. What if it had nothing to do with her and she had just made things so much worse.

'Calm down, Soph. No-one has died.'

Sofia looked at him closely and as he gazed back at her she knew that he was telling the truth. She swallowed the lump that had appeared in her throat.

'What is it, then?' She forced the words out. She wasn't sure that she wanted to know. She turned away from him for a moment, so that he couldn't see her face.

He had always said that he could read her like a book and she didn't want him to see what she feared she was giving away.

She still loved him. She always had and in that moment suspected that she always would.

'I've messed everything up and I've made you unhappy,' Jack said. His words were soft, too, but with the buzz of noise from the rest of the coach, Sofia was fairly sure that they weren't being overheard.

'I'm fine, Jack,' she said, knowing it wasn't exactly true but if the last few months had taught her anything, it was that she was strong enough to get through this and start over once again.

'I believe you, thousands wouldn't.' And now it was Sofia's turn to smile.

'Breaking up is painful,' Sofia said, glancing at him, 'for both of us.' She said the words that she hadn't believed at the time.

Jack had seemed totally unaffected when he had announced that he wanted a break but she could see now that he had simply hidden his pain better than she had.

'I can see that now and maybe we can be friends?' Sofia offered the olive branch that she thought Jack wanted to hear. She closed her eyes briefly and wondered if it would be more painful to never see Jack again or to have him in her life but only as a friend.

She didn't see the look on his face, which mirrored her own. When she looked at him again he was smiling.

'I'd like that, Sofia, if you think you can forgive me enough to try it?'

'Of course,' Sofia said with a confidence she didn't feel. 'Friends?' she said, holding out her hand. Jack looked at it for a heartbeat and then took it, shaking it firmly.

'Friends,' he said.

The noise of a man clearing his throat brought Sofia back to the here and now and the job at hand. Tino was politely trying to point out that they had arrived at the car park for the aqueduct and Sofia had failed to do her tour guiding bit.

'I have to . . . ' she started to say and

113

indicated the microphone with a nod of her head.

'Go for it,' Jack said and Sofia shifted back into her seat, picked up the microphone and started to give her introductory talk.

Behind Jack, Barbs Turner smiled thoughtfully and looked across the aisle to Greta, who smiled back. The exchange of smiles seemed to say it all. Those two young people needed a few nudges in the right direction and Greta and Barbs had made a wordless pact to help them.

The Other Woman

The coach pulled up back at the hotel just as Sofia was finishing her explanation of what they would be doing the next day.

'So, tomorrow morning we'll be aiming to leave at ten o'clock so that we will be in our next location near Monserrat by midday. Please bring your suitcases down to the lobby where Tino will load them on to the coach for you.

'The hotel in Monserrat will be providing lunch tomorrow and then you will have the afternoon to explore the town before we head up to the monastery on Wednesday.'

Sofia stepped off of the coach and watched the rest disembark. Jack was the last to get up from his seat.

'That was a great tour. I can see why you love this place,' he said as he moved to stand beside her. 'I don't think I've seen the real Spain when I've visited my holiday destinations with my folks.'

'It's a little different from the Costa del Sol.' Sofia smiled. She had told Jack so much about Spain and he had listened in the kind of tolerant way you do when you love someone but aren't really interested in what they are talking about.

'I may have to see if I can get them on to a tour. I think my dad would love it.'

'I suspect if I ask nicely I might be able to get them the friends and family discount.' Sofia could feel herself flush a little. They would have been family, if things are gone as they had both planned, until Jack changed his mind. 'I mean since we are going to be friends,' she added hurriedly.

'I know what you meant,' Jack said and he smiled at her as he walked past and into the hotel.

Sofia took a moment to compose herself. It wasn't as if she thought that being friends would be easy but she was going to need to be careful about what she said to avoid making herself and Jack uncomfortable.

Something told her it would be some time before either of them would feel entirely relaxed navigating the friend-ship thing. She headed straight for her office and her phone rang as soon as she sat down.

'Hola, Maria. How are you?'

'I am good but what I want to hear about is you? We have had no cancella-tions so I assume he is still there?' Maria put an emphasis on the word 'he' which told Sofia that she was less than impressed with Jack's behaviour.

'He is and we've had a talk. We're going to try to be friends.'

Maria snorted and Sofia knew her opinion before she said it.

'My darling, two people who have been in love cannot be friends. It is not possible. The old feelings that you think are gone, never are and they will rise up when you least want them to. You at least, I think, are still in love with him?'

Her tone was gentler now and Sofia wished that Maria was there with her. A hug right now wouldn't go amiss.

'I have to try, Maria. He looked so sad today.'

'He look sad because he is a fool!' Maria said sharply. 'He let you go, broke your heart and now he is sorry. It is too late, is it not?'

'Of course,' Sofia said, knowing that was what her cousin wanted to hear, although she wasn't sure that was the truth.

'You don't let him play with your heart again, Sofia. Promise me?'

'I promise.'

'Good. Then I need to talk to you about the hotel bookings.'

After they had finished with business, Sofia hung up. She had made a promise to Maria and in truth it was just a reflection of the promise she had made herself. But the problem was trying to be friends with Jack was going to be difficult, particularly when her heart wanted so much more.

She couldn't go back to Jack and say that she didn't want to be friends. She couldn't see him look so sad and hurt as he had that morning. No, what she needed to do was be careful, guard her heart and her emotions. Jack wanted them to be friends and she wanted — needed — to move on.

* * *

That evening at dinner, Sofia set out with her new plan fresh in her mind. She *could* be friends with Jack. This job had taught her how to get on with just about anyone and Jack was really no different.

Admittedly, none of the other people she had taken on the tour had ever broken her heart but that was something she didn't want to dwell on.

She made no comment when she realised that once again the only spare seat was with the Whiteheads, Mrs Turner and Jack. If this was how her guests wanted it to be then she would go along with it.

Sofia took her seat and smiled around at the table.

'Well, I hope you have all enjoyed your day,' she said and was greeted with smiles and 'Oh, yes.'

'I'm looking forward to Monserrat,' Tony said eagerly. 'I understand that much of it has had to be rebuilt but there are some parts that have survived Napoleon.'

'I'm sure Sofia wants to save her Monserrat speech for tomorrow, Tony,' Greta said, placing her hand over her husband's. 'Why don't we talk about something else?'

Sofia wasn't sure if she had imagined it but she thought she saw Greta and Barbs exchange glances. But the looks were gone as soon as they had arrived and Sofia decided that she might be getting a little paranoid.

'Where did you go to university, Sofia?' Greta asked with an air of innocence that made Sofia wonder if her initial assumptions had been right.

If she said where she had studied then they were bound to ask Jack which would make it impossible to avoid telling Barbs that they had been at university together.

'I studied at York,' Sofia said, grateful that the waiter had appeared with their wine order and offered a little distraction. 'Spanish and business studies,' Sofia added, hoping to take the conversation off on a different track.

'I studied at York, too,' Jack added before any more questions could be asked. Sofia wasn't sure whether she should be glad that he had taken control of the conversation or concerned about what he was about to say.

'Sofia and I were there at the same time.' He looked at Sofia now as if asking for permission. Sofia nodded slightly.

'She is one of the reasons I came on the tour.'

Sofia's eyes went wide and she stared down at her bread roll, pretending to focus on tearing it into small pieces and smothering it with butter. What was he doing?

'Sofia talked about this part of Spain a lot and I always fancied visiting it. So, when I heard about the tour from one of our mutual friends, I thought I would come along and see for myself.'

'A reunion of sorts, then?' Barbs asked.

Sofia looked at Jack, who seemed to have decided that this was the point he was going to stop talking.

'I guess so,' Sofia said, trying to keep her voice light. 'Jack and I studied different subjects. He was doing his paramedic course and I was doing mine.

'It was quite a surprise when he arrived and I realised who he was. Jack Brown is such a common name.' Sofia realised that she was babbling and reached for her glass of wine to give her a reason to stop talking.

'Well, I think it must be nice to have someone of your own age on the tour to talk with. Save you from all us old fuddy-duddies,' Tony said and Sofia was fairly sure he remained oblivious to any history between her and Jack.

'I enjoy everyone's company,' Sofia said diplomatically. 'I love meeting new people and hearing their stories.'

She had hoped that Tony might pick up on this hint and launch into one of his, which from previous experience told Sofia that he could probably entertain them through the starter and main course at least but Tony just smiled at her and nodded. There was silence then as if everyone were expecting someone else to speak.

'Well, I have a story about Mr Turner that I think you might find amusing,' Barbs offered and the rest of the table agreed and listened carefully to a story about Mr Turner, a ladder and a cat stuck up their chimney. Soon the party had relaxed and even Sofia found herself laughing at the funny tale.

'So, young Jack, is there a lovely lady in your life?'

The women at the table froze. Sofia

had a spoonful of Santiago tart in one hand and she had to put it down, knowing that she would not be able to eat it.

A quick glance up told her that Jack felt the same. He didn't answer but instead shovelled a mouthful of his own dessert into his mouth so that he wasn't able to speak, at least not in polite society.

'Tony, really!' Greta said, clearly exasperated. Tony seemed to have no idea what he had done wrong and looked around the table, taking in each of the faces. 'Young people don't like to be quizzed on their love life. It's private!' she added.

'Then who is Annabel?' Tony said, his confusion only growing as his wife glared at him.

Sofia looked at Jack whose face was a mask of shock.

'Annabel is . . . is a friend,' Jack said.

'Sounded like more than that to me, old chap,' Tony said winking at Jack who now looked horrified and was avoiding Sofia's gaze.

Sofia tried to look as if she was mildly interested and totally unaffected by this announcement but she knew that she wouldn't be able to keep the act up for long as her mind raced with possibilities. She felt in her pocket for her mobile.

'If you'll excuse me, I need to take this. It's the office.' Sofia knew that the rest of her party were unlikely to be fooled by a fake phone call but she could think of no other way to escape from the table.

'Of course, dear,' Mrs Turner said and the sympathy in her face was such that Sofia knew she couldn't hold her feelings in for a moment longer and she walked from the dining-room as quickly as she dared.

No More Games

Sofia walked as fast as she could across the main reception, avoiding eye contact and trying to look as though she had somewhere very important to be. She did, of course — she needed to get to her room before she started to cry.

Who was Annabel? Was she Jack's girlfriend? And if she was, why had Jack come to speak to her? Thoughts chased around in her head as she closed her room door behind her and slid across the bolt for good measure.

The housekeepers didn't come in the evening but even so she didn't want to risk being disturbed. She didn't want anyone to see her misery.

Why hadn't he told her about Annabel? She was clearly someone important. Clearly someone who meant a lot to Jack. If Tony had thought there was something going on when he had proved to be quite immune to the presence of such things, then Annabel had to be Jack's girlfriend.

It made even less sense then, as to why Jack had come. Perhaps he had told Annabel about Sofia and she had told him that he should make some sort of amends.

Sofia threw herself down on her bed and pulled her pillow over her head. If Jack had been prompted by Annabel to come all this way to apologise, well, then Sofia didn't think she would ever be able to look Annabel in the face. Annabel must think she was pathetic and unable to stand up for herself.

Sofia was just considering screaming into her pillow when another thought occurred to her. What if Annabel had ended things with Jack and that was why he was here?

Sofia threw the pillow on the floor and sat bolt upright. Was he here because he was on the rebound? Maybe he didn't want to be alone and so he thought that Sofia would just come running back if he turned up? The thought made the upset fade and her anger flare.

Wow, he must think so little of her if he thought that his half-hearted and quite frankly hurtful semi-apology would be enough to win her back. Maybe he thought playing the wounded party would have the right effect?

She glared at her own reflection in the mirror. If he had thought that, then Sofia had proved him right. The moment he looked sad and sorrowful she had felt so guilty that she had allowed herself to forget everything that had gone before and to hold out an olive branch. She had suggested that they try to be friends. Jack had cheered up at that. He probably thought it was the first step to winning her back.

Sofia walked up and down in the small room as she tried to process everything she had learned. It had been such a strange, up-and-down day but she finally felt like she knew where she stood — and more importantly, that she had figured out Jack's game.

A small part of her tried to suggest that she speak to Jack, rather than jumping to conclusions. But Sofia squashed the voice back down. She had worked so hard to put her life back together, to create a new life and so it was time that she heeded Maria's warning and not allow herself to get sucked back in, especially if it was just a game.

Maybe Jack was trying to make Annabel jealous and she was just a part of his plan to win her back.

All she needed to do now was work out how she was going to handle this. It wasn't in her nature to play games.

*　　★　　★

The next morning, Sofia was up early so that she could have breakfast and be ready to greet her guests. This was part of the plan that she had formulated overnight. Firstly, to keep busy and focus on her job and secondly to behave as if the day before hadn't happened.

She was going to treat Jack like any other guest. She would be friendly and polite but nothing more. It seemed that would be the best way to avoid playing any games he might be involved in and hopefully give the message that she was interested in nothing more than being friends.

In truth, that probably would end when the tour ended, since she couldn't see how being friends with her ex-boyfriend and his new girlfriend could ever work out well for any of them.

And if Jack was on the rebound? Well, she wasn't about to put herself through all that heartache again, particularly not if he was still in contact with Annabel, which had to mean that relationship wasn't over.

Sofia greeted her guests and relieved them of their luggage. Tino was hard at work loading the suitcases on to the coach.

'Good morning, dear. How are you this morning?' Barbs Turner had parked her red wheeled suitcase next to the others and was looking at Sofia with concern.

'I'm good, thank you, and how are you?' Sofia was impressed with how normal she managed to sound. She could feel Barbs studying her and so kept her smile firmly in place. Barbs nodded, seemingly satisfied.

'Will you be joining us for breakfast?'

'Not this morning, but thank you for the offer. I need to make sure everything is organised so I had my breakfast early.'

'I see. Well perhaps we can persuade you to join us for lunch at our next hotel.'

'That would be lovely,' Sofia said before she could come up with an excuse as to why she shouldn't. She always tried to eat with the guests if she was invited and she wasn't about to change that just because of Jack's presence.

All of the other guests were in the dining-room having breakfast when Jack finally appeared. He was carrying a large rucksack and Sofia couldn't help wondering if he had timed his arrival to miss all the other guests.

'Just leave your bag here and I'll see that it gets on the coach,' Sofia said, studying her clipboard more closely than was absolutely necessary. 'You'd better be quick or you will miss breakfast.'

'I'm not very hungry,' Jack said, not moving.

Sofia knew that if her plan was going to work she needed to look at him and pretend that nothing was wrong.

'We'll be on the coach for a couple of hours with no planned stops so it might be best to at least have a drink.'

'I need to talk to you,' Jack said, ignoring Sofia's suggestion.

'I'll be filling everyone in on today's programme when we are on the coach, so perhaps it can wait until then?' Sofia knew that wasn't what Jack wanted to talk to her about but she also knew that she didn't want to hear about Annabel or any kind of excuses or explanations. She couldn't afford to get upset — she had a job to do.

Jack said nothing but Sofia was rescued from the awkward silence by Tino reappearing and asking her a question in Spanish. By the time she had replied, Jack had gone.

Sofia felt a stab of guilt. For a person who didn't like playing games, particularly with other people's feelings, she couldn't help thinking that was exactly what she was doing. She sighed.

'You OK, Sofia?' Tino asked as he pulled the handles out on two suitcases.

'Fine, Tino. Thanks. Just thinking about all the things I need to do today.'

Tino nodded but his eyes were narrowed in that way he had when he wasn't sure she was being honest. Sofia smiled and Tino walked away, pulling the suitcases along behind him.

Sofia took a moment to close her eyes. Life had become so complicated in the last few days and she found herself wishing that the tour was over, so that Jack could go home, back to Annabel, and she could try to forget that these two weeks ever happened.

When Sofia climbed on board the coach she found that Barbs Turner had assumed Jack's seat. Sofia did a quick head count to make sure that she had all her guests and then let Tino know that they were ready to leave.

Jack was sitting at the back of the coach, in a gesture which seemed to send the message that he wanted to be as far away from her as possible. Sofia felt a stab of pain which she tried to ignore, telling herself it was for the best.

Once she had welcomed the guests on board, explained the route they would be taking and given them the estimated time of arrival, Sofia relaxed back into her seat. She tried to be happy that she wouldn't have to look at Jack feeling sorry for himself or be tempted to speak to him.

'May I?' Barbs asked, indicating the seat next to Sofia.

'Of course,' Sofia said, thinking that having someone to distract her might help.

'I know that you said you were fine but I just wanted to check, after everything that happened at dinner last night.'

Sofia blinked. This was not the kind of distracting conversation she had been hoping for.

'I'm fine, really. How are you enjoying the tour so far?'

'It's been wonderful. Mr Turner would have loved it and so I'm glad I came.'

Sofia smiled, feeling a little sad that Barbs was having to take the trip alone.

'Well, I'm very glad you came.'

Sofia was rewarded with a smile.

'Now, I know it's none of my business but I overheard Jack on the phone with this Annabel person and I have to say I didn't draw the same conclusions as Tony Whitehead.' Barbs seemed quite put out that Tony had managed to put his foot in it so spectacularly.

'Please don't worry about that. Anything between Jack and me is in the past.' Sofia decided at the moment that there was no point in pretending to Barbs, who seemed to have the whole situation sussed out.

'If you say so, dear,' Barbs said, in the kind of voice that Sofia's mum used, which meant 'I hear your words but I don't believe one of them.'

Sofia didn't really know what to say to that but Barbs seemed happy to change the subject and so they chatted happily for the two hours it took to get to their next hotel in Monserrat.

A Tangled Web

With all the guests settled in their rooms and getting ready for lunch, Sofia was able to make her way to her own room. She had barely closed the door when there was a soft knock. There was no way to know who it was and so Sofia pulled the door open, wondering if one of her guests had an issue with their room.

Jack was standing in the doorway. When he didn't say anything, Sofia thought that she had better get in first.

'Is there a problem with your room?' she asked.

Jack shook his head.

'I'm next door,' he said and Sofia blinked in surprise, thinking that she might ask Maria to ensure their rooms were far apart for the next hotel.

'OK. I expect I can get that changed if you are unhappy with that?' All Sofia wanted to do was grab a quick shower before the lunch was served but at the rate this conversation was going it wasn't going to happen.

'My room's fine,' Jack said and he looked glum. Yesterday that had made Sofia concerned but right now she just wished he would get to the point, and quickly, so that she could take that shower.

'Then is there something else I can help you with?' Sofia tried to keep her voice even but knew she was losing that battle.

'I don't want to bother you.'

'It's no bother,' Sofia said, forcing her best smile on to her face, 'but I can't help you unless you can tell me what the problem actually is.'

'It's about Annabel.'

Sofia had to fight the urge to slam the door in his face. It was a strong desire but she knew that it would be a mistake. Reacting like that would only make things worse and it was likely that she would end up having to have this conversation at some point anyway.

'I'm not sure there is much I can do for Annabel, unless she is joining us as a guest?' Sofia knew that she sounded snarky but couldn't seem to help it. This had to be part of the game and it was a game that Sofia had promised herself she wouldn't play.

'She's not a guest,' Jack said, looking confused as if this conversation was turning out how he expected. Well, that makes two of us, Sofia thought.

'I wanted to explain . . . about Annabel.'

'There's no need. It's really none of my business,' Sofia said, taking a step back into her room and hoping that the conversation was over.

'It's about what Tony said. He must have got the wrong end of the stick somehow.'

This caused a flare of memory in Sofia, of her conversation with Barbs, who had said something similar.

'Well, like I said, it doesn't matter if he did. Your relationship with Annabel is nothing to do with me, so it's fine.'

'Aren't you even going to let me explain?' Jack said, a tinge of anger in his voice.

'I would but you seem to be taking a long time to get to the point, if there is one, and I was hoping to get a shower in before lunch.'

'Right, well, in that case I won't take up any more of your time.'

Jack was gone before Sofia could say anything. He swiped his hotel key card and disappeared into the room next door. The lift at the end of the corridor pinged and Sofia ducked back inside before she could be caught by any other guests.

Closing the door behind her, she wondered why, after every conversation with Jack, she ended up feeling sorry for him or guilty about the way she had behaved. Maybe she could make more of an effort to hear him out? If she did, maybe they could all move on?

With a sigh, she walked into the bathroom. She would catch him later, maybe after lunch, when the rest of the tour had the free time to explore the village. Then she would ask him to tell her whatever he had to say and then hopefully that would be the end to this sorry chapter.

★   ★   ★

After everyone had eaten lunch, Sofia gave a brief overview of the rest of the day.

'I have a map for each of you although, to be honest, Castellbell isn't so big that you would get lost without it. If you head up to the north end of the town you can see the mountains of Monserrat in the distance.

'Tomorrow we will be catching the train which will take us up the mountain to the monastery but for today, you are free to explore or relax.

'We'll spend the whole day up in the mountains tomorrow and so it can be quite tiring, so feel free to make use of the facilities here at the hotel.'

Sofia handed out the maps and answered questions. Jack was sitting at the back and didn't appear to be paying much attention.

Sofia wasn't sure whether he didn't have plans to explore the town or if he was just making a point of ignoring her. When the other guests had filtered out she decided that now was a good time.

'Jack?' she said standing next to the small table he was sitting at.

Jack barely grunted in acknowledgement which almost made Sofia decide to leave him to it. But no, she wanted this dealt with. She wanted to get back to enjoying her job, not worrying about what Jack might say or do next.

'I thought perhaps now, we could talk about Annabel? If you still want to.'

'Is there any point?' Jack said with a moody shrug of his shoulders.

Sofia felt her temper flare but caught it in time.

'It's up to you,' Sofia said, feeling the need to make it clear that it didn't matter to her one way or the other, even though she had to admit that she did harbour a sort of morbid curiosity to find out the whole truth of the matter. 'But I have time now if you want to chat. Otherwise I will probably be too busy,' she added, hoping that would encourage him to get on with it.

'Annabel is not my girlfriend,' he said bluntly.

'OK,' Sofia said, thinking that she had been partially right. Perhaps Annabel had ended things and Jack decided that he would go back to his 'safe bet'. The idea of being anyone's safe bet did nothing for her temper.

'Was that it, or did you want to say something else?' she added and knew that she sounded irritable but she had had enough.

'There's no need to be like that. I'm trying to explain something,' Jack muttered.

'I'm sorry, I'm just hoping you might get to the point.' Any time in the next few hours would be good, Sofia thought to herself, wishing there was some way to make this move any faster.

'Maybe I've made it already,' Jack said, standing up. Sofia took a step backwards. He looked angry and she knew that she had not helped the matter but still, what did he have to be so cross about?

'In that case, if you'll excuse me I have some work to do,' Sofia said, forcing herself to look him in the eye and show him that she was not impressed by his outburst and then she walked from the room.

'Sofia . . . '

'Annabel is not your girlfriend. I got that. Although what it has to do with me I've no idea.'

'That is what I am trying to explain to you,' Jack said, running his hands through his hair.

Sofia stopped walking and put her hands on her hips.

'OK, well, go on, then.'

Jack looked as though he wasn't sure if it was worth carrying on, considering the reception he was getting, and Sofia felt another stab of guilt.

This was all on Jack. She hadn't asked him to come to Spain, to come on her tour, unannounced.

He had just turned up and now that he was here, he didn't seem able to decide what it was he wanted to say. And Sofia was getting to the point that she didn't want to hear it.

His presence had stirred up a lot of what she thought was in the past and had worked hard to keep it there.

'Jack, I'm happy to listen to what you have to say,' she said, hoping she was achieving a reasonable tone, 'but I really do have work to do.'

'I think I'm probably wasting my time,' he said before standing up, 'but don't say I didn't try.'

Sofia was so stunned that she stayed standing where she was for some time. What that was supposed to mean, Sofia had no idea. She folded into the nearest seat.

She really did have work to do but it was hard to focus with Jack's words swirling around in her head. Every time they talked, she felt more confused than she was before.

She just couldn't figure out what was going on and now it seemed like he was prepared to tell her. It was infuriating!

'Sofia? Sorry to interrupt.' One of her guests was standing next to her and looked concerned about disturbing her.

'I'm sorry. I was day dreaming,' Sofia said. What she needed to do was focus on work. There were ten days of the tour left and she was sure she could manage to stay out of Jack's way for that length of time. 'What can I do for you, Mr Banks?'

Turning Into a Nightmare

It didn't take long for Sofia to sort out the Banks's issue with their room. Mrs Banks was a light sleeper and they were at the front of the hotel and so didn't think she would be able to sleep with the noise from the road. Sofia had swiftly arranged for a room change and the Banks had gone off happy. She was standing at the main reception desk, just filling in the last of the paperwork, when a shadow fell over her.

'Can we talk?'

Sofia knew who it was without looking up from her paperwork.

'Of course,' she said, even though it was the last thing she felt like saying, or doing for that matter. 'Perhaps we should go through to the bar?'

'Perfect, I'll get us both a drink,' Jack said before disappearing off in the direction. That wasn't exactly what

Sofia had meant. A quick chat was unlikely if they had drinks to go with it.

She wasn't permitted to drink whilst at work, other than a glass of wine with dinner and so she finished what she was doing and hurried after Jack before he could order her something alcoholic.

Jack was sitting in the far corner and a waitress was bringing over two coffees. Well, that was a good sign, Sofia thought. She took a seat opposite Jack and tried to push all her personal feelings from her mind.

She needed to listen and not interrupt, however much she might want to, or this would turn out exactly like their last conversation. She had promised herself she would be the grown up, whatever Jack might have to say and now she was going to have to put the theory into practice.

Sofia helped herself to the complementary biscuit. She wasn't particularly hungry but needed to do something with her hands.

She didn't want to give Jack the

impression that she was anything other than happy to listen to whatever he had to say.

Jack didn't seem to be in a hurry to talk and Sofia wasn't sure whether that was a general reluctance or he just wasn't that concerned about it.

'So . . . ' Sofia said after minutes had passed and neither of them had said a word.

'Yes . . . Annabel,' Jack said and Sofia could now see that he was in fact reluctant to tell her about Annabel and alarm bells rang in Sofia's head. Surely the only reason he would feel that way was if he knew she wouldn't like what he was about to say.

'Annabel is just a friend,' Jack said finally. Sofia nodded expectantly but when Jack said nothing more, she thought that the coffees were probably a tad unnecessary since the conversation was going to be that short.

'Right,' Sofia said feeling a little more confused than before.

'She helped me a lot after everything

finished between you and me.'

Sofia raised an eyebrow. She couldn't help it. Jack was the one who had ended it after all. He had said that he needed to, that it was the right thing for them both, so why had he needed a shoulder to cry on?

She had been the one who had been totally taken by surprised and over-whelmed by shock and grief and worse than that, rejection.

'She was a good listener and helped me to understand, you know, what I was thinking.'

Sofia hadn't felt that kindly towards this Annabel and now she was feeling rising anger. It seemed now that Annabel had ulterior motives. Surely her idea of helping was to convince Jack that he had made the right choice so that she could have him herself!

Sofia shifted in her seat, not sure that she wanted to hear any more and then a terrible thought hit her.

'So,' she asked as casually as she could, 'where did you meet Annabel?'

Now it was Jack's turn to shift in his seat, along with looking anywhere other than at Sofia. He didn't need to say it, Sofia had figured out exactly who Annabel was.

'Annabel King? From my class at university?' Sofia didn't add the fact that Annabel seemed to have taken an instant dislike to her. In fact, she had seemed to go out of her way to ensure that Sofia and the rest of the class knew exactly what she thought.

Sofia had tried repeatedly to be friendly but it was no use. Annabel's mind had been set and it seemed there had been no changing it. Annabel's presence had been the one sour note to a very enjoyable three years, a bit like a splinter under your skin that you couldn't get rid of.

'Annabel,' Sofia said again, not quite believing it. Of all the people that Jack could have gone to for support, he had gone to Annabel, the person who seemed to like Sofia least in this world, and Sofia still had no idea why.

Sofia hadn't even realised that Jack had known Annabel that well. It wasn't as if they had all socialised together.

'We happened to cross paths one day and got talking,' Jack said. 'She had some things going on in her life, like I did in mine and it sort of went from there.'

Sofia swallowed. Had Jack come all this way to tell her that he was now friends with Annabel? She shook her head. That didn't make sense.

'I know that you and Annabel weren't close but she is a lovely person when you get to know her.'

'I'm sure she is. It's unfortunate that she never seemed interested in getting to know me.'

'Well, she's sorry for that. In fact, when she knew I was coming over to see you she wanted me to explain, you know, on her behalf.'

'Jack, I'm happy to listen to what you have got to say but if Annabel wants to make things right, she needs to tell me herself.'

Sofia stood up before she realised that she'd done it. This whole situation seemed to be turning into a nightmare.

It was bad enough when she thought Jack had met someone else but now that she knew that someone was Annabel King, well, she didn't think she could take any more. It was all too much and all she wished was that she could rewind life to a few days ago, before Jack had reappeared in her life and thrown it all back into chaos.

'Come on, Sofia, don't be like that. It was a while ago and . . . '

'Like I said Jack, Annabel needs to speak to me herself, not use you as a go between. We aren't teenagers any more. And besides, why would she want to make peace with me now?'

Jack shrugged.

'She was hoping we could all be friends.'

Sofia stared. She couldn't imagine trying to be friends with Jack and having Annabel around at the same time. Annabel's attitude to her made her feel as if she wasn't quite up to scratch and there was no way she wanted to go back to feeling like that.

'When you next speak to Annabel, please tell her that the past is in the past and she shouldn't concern herself with it any more.

'I'm sorry. I've just remembered some things I need to attend to for the tour of Monserrat tomorrow.'

Jack looked unconvinced.

'Of course,' he said. 'Perhaps we can catch up after dinner this evening.'

Sofia nodded, not certain that her voice would be steady if she tried any other answer, and left as quickly as she dared, feeling Jack watching her go.

A Moving Experience

Sofia had avoided dinner and instead she had ordered in food. She told herself it was so she could catch up on e-mails but she knew it was because she didn't want to see Jack. She shook her head as she scooped up a forkful of paella.

Annabel King, the person at university who had seemed to take an instant dislike to Sofia, with no explanation! That Annabel had been advising and supporting Jack after he broke up with her. She could only imagine what Annabel might have said about her. The thought was putting her off her dinner.

What she couldn't understand was Jack's attitude. She had spent many an evening with him, upset over the latest slight that Annabel had sent in her direction.

How did he think that she would take

the news that he and Annabel were now best friends? It was almost worse than if they were dating!

Sofia stared at her dinner, all thoughts of hunger gone now. She could not figure Jack out. It made more sense, his sudden appearance and the chaos he had wrought in her life since his arrival, if Annabel was now his personal advisor. But why now, after all that time? He could have sent her a text or even called her if he wanted to talk.

Why come all the way over here, and spend all that money on a tour that was not exactly designed for his interests? It had to be Annabel. Seemingly she wasn't content with her efforts to make Sofia's life miserable during their years at university. Now she seemed to want to continue with her game.

Sofia started to walk up and down the room. Jack was clearly in contact with Annabel, if the overheard phone call was anything to go by, which meant that Jack had likely relayed Sofia's every reaction.

Sofia looked at her reflection in the mirror. That meant only one thing. She needed to act as if none of this situation bothered her, work hard at trying to be friends with Jack and not let any of her feelings show.

Surely Annabel would get bored if she wasn't getting the reaction she was hoping for? That was certainly the advice that Sofia's mum had given her every time she had phoned home upset about Annabel's latest antics and it was always good to take her mum's advice.

Tino pulled the coach up outside the train station that housed the train that would take them all up into the mountains. Sofia hopped off and went over to collect their group tickets before returning to the coach.

'We are booked on the next train so if you would like to follow me? There is only one stop so if I could ask you all to find a seat and then get off at the top. I will be standing outside the train station and will wave this.' Sofia demonstrated by waving her Garcia

Tours flag in the air.

'So please come and find me and once we are all together we will start our walking tour.'

The train was busy and Sofia jumped on last, once she had made sure that all her guests were aboard. There were no seats left so she stood and looked out of the window at the amazing mountain backdrops.

Monserrat was one of her favourite places on the tour. She loved the history of the place and the idea that people had been coming on pilgrimages for hundreds of years.

Every day at 11 o'clock there was a short service that was open to all, and the cathedral choir or the choir of monks would sing. It was a magical experience that she always encouraged her guests to attend whether they were churchgoers or not.

Standing outside the train station with her small flag in the air, Sofia saw Jack help Tony off the train. Whilst she had been doing her best to politely avoid him, she was glad that he was going to see Monserrat.

It was such a special place and of all the things she had talked to him about when they were together, this was the place she had longed to bring him the most.

When all the guests were gathered, Sofia started to walk and explain the history of the place, through its destruction by Napoleon's men to the glorious rebuild of Santa Maria de Montserrat, its huge Benedictine abbey which sat cut into the mountains.

Sofia's clear love of the place had her audience enthralled and time passed quickly until they found themselves standing outside the carved edifice that would lead them into the basilica itself.

'As I have said before, I would encourage each of you to attend the short service which will begin shortly. After that you are free to explore or take the funicular up to the top of the mountain. Please be back here at two-thirty so that we can take our behind-the-scenes tour.

'You all have my mobile number so if you have any problems or difficulties then please don't hesitate to call me.'

Sofia smiled as the group joined the queue to get into the basilica. She joined the tail end and found that it was nearly full, with only a few seats left. She stood at the back, declining offers of seats. She had the opportunity to attend the service every few weeks but for many of her guests it would be the first and only time they could enjoy the moment.

More people joined her, filtering in all the time, and so Sofia found herself shifted into a corner behind the last pew, with Jack standing next to her. She knew she couldn't ignore his presence, particularly as more people were trying to enter the basilica which meant they were standing shoulder to shoulder, so she looked up and smiled briefly, before turning her head in the direction of the priest, who had started to speak.

As always happened, Sofia was transported away by the words and the music. The rest of congregation also seemed to have fallen under the spell and the silence, in between words and song, was peaceful.

When the service was over and the boys' choir started to file through the door at the back of the basilica, the congregation started to disperse too. Since she didn't want to fight through the tightly bunched queue of people, Sofia stayed where she was and enjoyed the peaceful sensation she always found here.

'That was beautiful,' Jack said.

'It's hard to describe it. You have to come for yourself,' Sofia said softly.

'I thought I could imagine it from all those times you spoke about it but, like you say, you have to come for yourself.'

Sofia smiled. She knew she wasn't following her own plan but it did feel good to share the moment with Jack.

'I was going to sit down at the front. You can get a view of the altar and I can point out the statue of the abbey's patron saint, if you like.'

Jack dragged his eyes away from

studying his surroundings.

'I'd like that, if you don't mind?'

Sofia nodded.

'I don't mind,' she said before leading the way down the side aisle to the front of the basilica. There were spaces at the front where a few visitors sat in silent contemplation. Sofia sat down and Jack joined her. The altar and surrounding splendour needed no explanation so she remained quiet as his eyes took in the spectacle.

When Jack finally looked at her, she lifted a hand and pointed at the small window above the altar and together they watched as pilgrims from far and wide stood before the statue and placed their hand on the black orb that the Madonna held.

For those moments, it was as Sofia had always imagined it would be. They had talked tentatively that their honeymoon would take in this part of Spain and Sofia had longed to bring Jack here, to share her love of this place with him.

They sat for an age, and Sofia wondered if it was because neither of them wanted to break the spell. She wondered if Jack felt it too. They sat, side by side as if nothing had changed, when in fact everything had.

'I need to go and get some lunch before the tour this afternoon,' Sofia said when the bells tolled for one o'clock.

'Of course. I'll see you at the meeting spot later,' Jack said with a half smile but Sofia was sure she could detect sadness in his eyes.

'Why don't you join me?' Sofia said. She knew what she had promised herself but in that moment, in that place, she couldn't see what harm it would do to simply share lunch with him.

'I'd like that,' Jack said and together they walked down the side aisle and out into the sunshine.

No Further Forward

They made their way to one of the restaurants and ordered their food, and since the weather was warm, despite the fact that they were up in the mountains, Sofia led Jack out on to the upstairs patio where they could take in the amazing views.

'This really is an incredible place,' Jack said as he took his seat. 'I always imagined that the monks and priests would be terribly solemn but they look happy.' He looked up and caught Sofia's eye.

She smiled at him.

'That must sound like a foolish thing to say.'

'Not at all,' she replied, marvelling that their opinions were so in tune. 'I thought the same the first time I visited, but I think everyone who chooses to live here has a genuine affection for the place. The boys at the school seemed to love it, too. In fact, for Catalonians, it is seen as an ultimate privilege to win a place here.'

'I can imagine,' Jack said thoughtfully. 'What a view to have from your classroom window.'

'You should go up on the funicular and see the view from the top. It's amazing to see the monastery and the abbey from up there.'

Jack winced.

'Not sure about that.'

Sofia nodded as she remembered that Jack had one weakness and that was heights.

'I think you'd be fine when you got up there.' She tried to keep the smile from tugging at her lips but failed miserably.

'It's the getting up there that's the problem,' Jack said, eyeing the cable car crossed with train that moved up the steep side of the mountain. 'And it's not funny,' he pointed out, but he was smiling, too.

'Well, maybe it's best you just enjoy

the view from here.'

'Probably. It's going to be hard for you to leave here, I imagine?' Jack said and Sofia could feel his eyes studying her.

'No, not really. I have another tour immediately after this one so I'll be back in two weeks.'

'I meant Spain,' Jack said and now Sofia had an idea of what he was getting at.

'Who said I was leaving?' Sofia asked.

'I just thought when the season was over that you would come home.'

'Maybe I am home,' Sofia said, eyeing him over her cup of coffee.

Jack shifted in his seat and turned to gaze at the mountains.

'I guess I figured this was just one of the summer jobs.'

'It started out that way but I've enjoyed spending time with my Spanish side of the family. They've made me feel very welcome and like I belong.'

'But it's not really a career move, is it?' Jack said and he was leaning forward, his face serious. 'I mean, you had plans to be a top-level translator.'

Sofia felt herself stiffen under what could only be described as his judgement of her choices.

'Well, you would have to be the first to acknowledge that plans change.' Sofia's eyes flashed and knew that she should stop talking. If they continued like this it would just end in another argument. The truth was, she hadn't made up her mind. She knew she had an offer of a job in her uncle's office over the off season and she was considering taking it.

Jack looked wounded but seemed to shake it off.

'So, you're going to stay?' he asked.

'I'm not sure yet,' Sofia answered honestly although she felt that he had no right to ask her for her plans.

'You might not?'

'Like I said, I don't know.' Sofia made a show of looking at her watch. 'I need to head off to the meeting spot now. We have to be escorted on this part of the tour and I need to check everything is in place.'

'OK,' Jack said, 'I'll come with you.' He made to stand.

'It won't be particularly interesting — just paperwork to be completed. Why not have a look around and take in some more of the sights?'

Jack shrugged as if it meant nothing to him either way and so Sofia stood up from the table and walked away. When she was far enough away to risk it, she took a peek over her shoulder and her hunch was right. Jack was sitting staring at the mountain, with his mobile phone to his ear and Sofia was pretty sure she knew who he was talking to.

⋆   ⋆   ⋆

It had been a long day and all Sofia wanted was to kick off her shoes and have a long soak in the bath, preferably with a cup of tea and a good book but that was rarely on the agenda when she was working.

So instead, she rushed up to her

room and had a quick shower. It wasn't the same as a long bath but it would have to do under the circumstances. The tour would be travelling to Barcelona the following day and Sofia needed to double check that all the arrangements were in place.

Sofia had no office at this hotel and so instead had found a quiet spot in the bar. She was happy to be interrupted by her guests, after all that was what she was here for, but she couldn't help hoping that Jack would stay away.

He had assumed that her time in Spain was just an escape, an escape from her heartache. He had made her feel like she had run away, when in truth that was what Jack had done.

Sofia had tried to contact him but had nothing back and mutual friends had reassured her that Jack was fine but just needed space, whatever that was supposed to mean.

Her decision to come to Spain had been taken very seriously. She had always wanted to experience Spain as her dad had done growing up and to get to know that side of the family better than could be achieved by annual visits and the odd phone call. He had no right to judge her decisions.

If Jack had thought his presence would be enough to sway her decision to leave Spain and go back to the UK then he was wrong. If anything, it had had the opposite effect. It made her more determined to continue to develop a life here, where her new friends and family wanted her to be around, unlike Jack.

Did he expect that he could just turn up and convince her to walk away from all she had built up since their split? He was right, of course — in the long term she wanted to be a translator. Her dream would be working for somewhere like the UN, but there would be time for that later.

And besides, her dreams were just that, hers. She would be the one to decide what she was going to do with her life. It had nothing to do with Jack.

'Sofia, about earlier . . . '

Sofia jumped, jolted from her thoughts, and blinked. At first, she thought she had imagined Jack's presence but no, there he was, standing in front of her.

'What about it?' Sofia asked, wishing she had decided to stay in her room and work, rather than come down and risk exactly this happening.

'I think you might have taken what I said the wrong way,' he said. He didn't sit down and Sofia suspected that her expression was enough to convey the message that he wasn't welcome.

'Really? It seemed to me that you were suggesting this was a job that was beneath me and that what I should do was return to the UK and get a proper job.'

Jack's face crumpled.

'Well, that wasn't what I meant.' He looked annoyed and Sofia didn't need a crystal ball to know where this conversation was going. She sighed.

'Fine, I misunderstood what you were trying to say. I'm sorry for my part in it.' Sofia looked up at him. 'Perhaps we can just move on without having to pick it all apart and analyse it.'

'Are you saying that's what you think I do?' Jack's face was set hard now and Sofia just wanted this conversation to be over.

'Sometimes I think you do,' Sofia said, going for what she hoped was a reasonable tone, but judging by the stony expression on Jack's face it wasn't being received that way. 'Sometimes we need to examine what we say but I'm just wondering if this time we could agree that there were some misunder-standings and move on.'

Jack was shaking his head.

'You are impossible,' he said between clenched teeth. Sofia raised an eyebrow and somehow both of her hands migrated to her hips.

'I'm sorry that you feel that way,' Sofia said, doing her best not to rise to the criticism.

'There is clearly no point in trying to talk to you when you are in this kind of mood.'

Sofia opened her mouth to tell him exactly what she thought of his comments but didn't have a chance to speak as a group from the tour had appeared in the bar and were ordering coffees.

'Let me know when you are ready to listen,' Jack hissed quietly.

Sofia watched him leave, wondering how they had ever managed to have a complete and civil conversation. It should not have been a surprise that they had both changed so much over the last eight months.

After Jack's pronouncement, Sofia had spent many a night wondering if she knew him at all. The events of the past week were doing nothing to dispel those thoughts.

Sofia sighed and tried to focus on the e-mails in her account. One was from her mum, and reading her words always cheered her up. She wondered whether she should tell her that Jack was on her tour. Normally she told her mum everything but Sofia was pretty sure she knew what her reaction would be to the news. All she needed to do was survive another nine days and then Jack would go home and then she could tell her mum all about it.

The Best-laid Plans . . .

The tour had moved to its new base in Barcelona, where they would be staying at the same hotel for the remainder of the tour. This was good news for Sofia as it meant that she could go back to the small apartment she shared with Maria, rather than needing to stay in the hotel.

The hotel and her guests all had her phone number so she could be contacted in case of emergency.

It was late when she arrived home. She dumped her bags in her bedroom and walked to the kitchen in search of something to eat.

Maria was curled up on the sofa watching her favourite soap opera and so Sofia made herself a sandwich and then plonked herself down on the sofa next to her cousin.

Sofia knew better than to interrupt so

had to wait for the adverts before she knew it was safe to speak. As soon as the first advert started, Maria turned her attention to her cousin.

'All the guests are settled?' she asked, reaching over and helping herself to one of the crisps that Sofia had piled on her plate next to her sandwich.

'Hopefully. They have my number if there are any problems. It's good to be home.'

'Might that have something to do with Jack, your ex-boyfriend who has no doubt been making waves?' Maria asked and Sofia knew that she expected all the juicy details. She sighed.

'I just can't figure him out. I still don't know why he came, and all he seems to want to do is argue with me.'

Maria nodded in amusement and Sofia felt confused.

'Arguments are all about passion, Sofia. Surely I don't need to tell you that.'

'Trust me, these arguments have nothing to do with passion and everything to do with the fact that we don't seem to understand each other any more.'

'Pah,' Maria said dismissively. 'Why else would he come, except to try and make it up to you?' Maria helped herself to another crisp. 'But you of course will have no interest in that.'

'You know I don't,' Sofia said, putting her plate down. Her appetite seemed to leave her every time she thought about Jack. Maria watched the motion and raised an eyebrow.

'That's what you say but you behave like the opposite is true.'

'You don't need to worry about me. All I want is for this next week to be over and for Jack to go home so I can get back to my life without all the complications.'

'Uh-huh,' Maria said but she sounded unconvinced. The soap opera jingle started and Sofia knew that Maria would want to give it her full attention.

'I'm going to have a bath.'

'OK, but we talk more when this is over?' Maria said, gesturing at the TV.

'I wouldn't expect anything less,'

Sofia said with a grin. It was good to be home and to have someone she could talk to about all this. She and Maria had started off as cousins but now Sofia felt more like they were sisters.

When Sofia returned, wrapped in her bath robe with her hair tied up in a turban, Maria had poured out two glasses of wine and found some chocolate.

'You always know exactly what I need,' Sofia said with a giggle.

'Of course I do, we are family!' Maria said, as if it were the most obvious thing in the world. 'Now you must tell me everything, even the things that you have told me before, I need to know what happened in order,' Maria said, patting the sofa seat beside her and offering Sofia a glass of wine.

Sofia accepted the wine and took a grateful sip before helping herself to a square of chocolate. When she felt suitably recharged, she told Maria the whole story.

'It makes no sense to me,' Sofia said as she finished her tale. 'One minute I think he is here because he is interested in trying again and the next he seems angry with me or exasperated. Then it feels as if he wants to apologise, for some reason.' Sofia shook her head, even saying it out loud to Maria hadn't made any more sense of it.

'He is a man,' Maria said as if that explained it all.

'I had noticed,' Sofia said dryly.

'What I mean,' Maria said pointedly, 'is that we are assuming his motives are complex. Men are much more simple than that.'

'So, what do you think he wants?' Sofia said, wondering if Maria, with the luxury of distance and no hurt feelings, had managed to figure it all out.

'I have no idea,' Maria said with a twinkle in her eye and they both dissolved into a fit of giggles.

'Well, you're a fat lot of help.'

'You need to ask him straight out,' Maria said pointing a finger at Sofia. 'You have not yet asked him, yes?'

'Well, not exactly, but he has had

plenty of opportunity . . . '

Maria cut her off with a dismissive wave of her hand.

'He will not take it! He is a man. You, *you* must take control. *You* must sit him down, tell him to hold his tongue and then ask him. Look him in the eye and ask him.'

'I can't!' Sofia said, horrified at the thought.

'You are a Garcia woman, of course you can!' Maria said triumphantly. 'You must put aside your Englishness and be Spanish! We Spanish women would not take what you have taken and so you must go to him and demand he tells you everything.'

Sofia took a bigger sip of wine.

'Maybe you're right.'

'Of course I am right.'

'I might not like what he has to say,' Sofia said thoughtfully.

'No doubt — but at least you will know and when you do, you can send him packing.'

'I just need to find the right time.'

Maria looked at her and Sofia knew that expression. It told her that Maria knew she was stalling and was not impressed.

'We have the city tour tomorrow. It's not the kind of conversation I can have on the coach,' Sofia protested.

'They have a few hours in the afternoon to explore our city, yes?'

Sofia nodded, knowing where this was going.

'Then you take him aside and you go somewhere quiet and you ask him.' Maria said as if it was all agreed and Sofia knew from experience that there was no point in arguing. She also knew that if she didn't do it, Maria was likely to step in and take matters into her own hands. No matter how confused her feelings were for Jack right now, she didn't think he deserved the full-blown wrath of Maria.

'Fine,' Sofia said with an exaggerated smile. 'Tomorrow I will invite him for a coffee and ask him.'

'You need to be very specific. You

know that men are not the smartest when it comes to matters of the heart.'

'Yes, yes. I will be very specific. Something along the lines of 'Why are you here?''

'Very good,' Maria said, seemingly satisfied. 'Now we watch a movie?'

★ ★ ★

The next day, after another pep talk from Maria, Sofia was at the hotel and waiting for the guests to come down to breakfast. She didn't think she had felt this nervous since her first tour. In her head she replayed the steps of the tour, anything to keep her mind off of Jack. She had thought about asking him at breakfast to meet her for coffee in the afternoon break, but decided that would only make her feel worse, being aware that Jack was probably wondering what was going on.

Sofia greeted each guest, smiling and saying all the right things, but her eyes kept flicking to the lift as she expected

Jack to arrive at any moment. All the guests had been eating for over 20 minutes and still there was no sign of Jack.

She frowned, wondering if he had decided to skip breakfast. At nine-thirty the tour guests were gathered in reception, ready to head out on foot for the first part of the Barcelona city tour and still there was no Jack.

'Sorry for the delay, ladies and gentlemen,' Sofia called out over the small crowd, 'but we are just waiting for one guest.'

Barbs Turner made her way through the group, her face looked concerned.

'Is everything OK, Mrs Turner?' Sofia asked

Barbs Turner wrung her hands.

'I'm fine, dear. It's just that Jack said last night he wasn't sure if he would be able to come on the tour today. Something to do with work, he said. I'm surprised he didn't call you.'

Sofia tried to smile reassuringly. The last thing she wanted was to upset Mrs

Turner's holiday plans with her relationship dramas.

'I expect he phoned into the office. My mobile reception is sometimes a little off.'

Barbs smiled and looked a little less worried.

'If you'll excuse me I'll just step away and ring the office.' Sofia turned and walked away.

That was just typical, she finally had a plan to find out what was going on and the vital piece was now missing. Where was Jack? And what game was he playing? How could he possibly have an issue with work that needed dealing with? He was a paramedic, for goodness' sake. If his work needed him then he would have to fly home and surely, he hadn't done that? Had he?

Search for the Truth

A quick phone call to the office told Sofia that Jack hadn't been in contact. The reception desk had no records of him having checked out but there was no answer to his room phone.

Sofia felt a flash of worry and then irritation. It was just downright rude not to let her know he wasn't intending to come on the city tour. The least he could have done was leave her a message.

Now she had delayed the start of the tour for no reason other than his inability to think about anyone other than himself.

Sofia walked back over to the tour group.

'Right, folks. It seems one of our guests won't be joining us on the city tour this morning. I'm sorry for the delay but if you would like to follow me we will head out to our first stop which will be the Sagrada Familia, the work of Antoni Gaudi and his yet unfinished church.'

By mid afternoon the group had toured the Sagrada Familia, the Rambles and the Gothic Quarter and now Sofia had given the tour the rest of the afternoon to explore at their own pace before meeting back at the Sagrada Familia at five to walk back to the hotel.

With a few hours to fill, now that Jack was nowhere to be found, Sofia had thought about going shopping but her heart was simply not in it. When her mobile rang she was glad of the distraction but hoping that her guests had not had any problems.

'Hola,' Sofia answered. She didn't recognise the number and so it seemed the best approach.

'Sofia, it's Jack.'

Sofia said nothing. She wasn't sure what she was supposed to say.

'Look, I know I missed the tour . . . '

'Yes,' Sofia said cutting him off. 'It

would have been nice of you to have informed me. We waited for you. You delayed the start of the tour for the whole group, Jack. It's just common courtesy.'

'My apologies,' Jack said and he sounded like he meant it. 'Something unexpected happened and I needed to be somewhere else.'

Sofia frowned. If he was trying to be mysterious to intrigue her, it wasn't working since all she felt was slightly disgruntled.

'Really? You're on holiday, Jack. What exactly has come up that would keep you away from the tour?' Sofia stared at her own reflection in a shop window. 'It doesn't matter to me that you missed it but it would have been helpful for you to let me know, even if you just left a message for me.'

'I know and as I said I'm sorry about that. But I was wondering if we could meet up? I know the other guests have some free time to explore this afternoon.'

Sofia blinked. She hadn't expected him to invite her to meet for a conversation and somehow she felt wrong-footed by it. Then Maria's voice sounded in her mind, telling her that it didn't matter whose suggestion it was, just that it would be an opportunity once and for all for Sofia to ask him what was going on.

'OK, well, I'm near the Sagrada Familia, I'll wait for you here. There are plenty of cafés.'

'Sounds perfect. Just one question.'

'Yes?'

'What exactly is the Sagrada Familia and where is it?'

Sofia rolled her eyes.

'Head out of the hotel up the road to your right and I'll walk down and meet you.'

'Great!'

Sofia was nearly back to the hotel when she met Jack, who was walking towards her with a barely contained grin on his face. What he had to be so cheerful about, Sofia wasn't sure. All she wanted to do was find a quiet café, where they could order coffee and she could ask her question before she could get too distracted.

Jack seemed happy to walk together in silence, gazing at all the sights around him. Sofia had to fight her tour-guide urge to point out places of interest. Right now she wasn't a tour guide and she needed to stay focused.

She took them down a side street to a small café which had a yard area out the back. It was popular with the locals and so Sofia thought it was unlikely that anyone else from the tour would find them there.

She greeted the owner with a wave and walked through the café into the yard area, finding them a table tucked away in one corner. Once they had their drinks, Sofia took a deep breath.

'Why did you come here?' Sofia blurted out. Jack spoke at he same moment.

'I have something I want to tell you,' he said.

They looked at each other, expecting one of them to speak but when neither of them did, the both tried again, speaking over each other once more.

'Would you mind if I go first?' Jack said.

Sofia clenched her hands in her lap. If she let him speak she knew that she would never get to the bottom of things.

'I need to ask you a question, Jack. Just one and then I would be happy to listen to whatever you have to say.'

Jack studied her and then shrugged, leaning back in his chair and looking as though he was preparing himself for an unpleasant conversation.

'I need to know why you are here,' Sofia said, forcing the words out. She looked up at him expectantly.

'You agreed to meet me,' he said, more of a question than a statement. Sofia sighed.

'You know that's not what I mean.'

'Well, I think we both know how easy it is to be misunderstood.'

Sofia glared at him, she couldn't help it. Of course she could see the irony but it was clear that he was misunderstanding on purpose. It was infuriating.

'Jack, please, can you just answer this one simple question? I need to know.'

'I'm here because you are here,' he said, as if that was all Sofia needed to know.

'Yes, but why?' Sofia spoke each word slowly.

'That's actually connected to what I wanted to tell you.'

'Fine,' Sofia said, blowing out a breath in frustration. 'Why don't you go ahead?'

What she really wanted to ask was why he couldn't answer a simple straightforward question but she knew that if she pursued that they would just argue again.

Jack moved in his seat, crossed his legs and uncrossed them. Sofia said nothing. Jack was clearly nervous about whatever he had to tell her and if she made sympathetic noises, she was worried that he would never get to his point.

'I came to Spain to see you.'

Sofia nodded. He was saying the same thing but in a different way and it wasn't shedding any light on the matter as far as she was concerned.

'I wanted to see you, to see how you were doing after . . . after everything that happened.'

'You could have phoned or e-mailed,' Sofia said. She had planned to keep quiet until he finished but she needed to know. 'Nothing for eight months and then you turn up out of the blue. Did you think about me at all?'

'Of course I did!' Jack said hotly. 'I thought of nothing else!'

'I meant when you decided to come out here.' Sofia filed away his comment to think about later. Right now, she was on the path to answers and she wasn't going to stop until she got some.

'I didn't text or call because I was worried how you would respond,' Jack said, looking down.

'And so you thought ambushing me at work in a different country was the right answer?'

'No, I thought if I came on the tour you would have to speak to me ... ' Jack looked sheepish and Sofia could have laughed if she wasn't still trying to work out exactly what was happening.

'I heard nothing from you for months, Jack — not a peep — and I'm supposed to believe that you suddenly decided that you had to see me?'

'Just because I wasn't in touch didn't mean that I didn't think about you a lot.'

Sofia stared at him as she tried to work out what was going on in Jack's head.

'Generally, if you spend that much time thinking about someone, you make an effort to reach out.' What she didn't add was 'especially when that person was heartbroken and missing you like crazy.' She didn't want to say those things. She knew if she did, she would most likely cry.

'That's what Annabel kept telling me.'

Jack looked at her and Sofia knew that he was checking for her reaction so she kept her face smooth.

'What did Annabel tell you?' she asked coolly.

'Well, aside from calling me all kinds of idiot for letting you go . . . ' Sofia raised an eyebrow in surprise. That didn't sound like the Annabel she knew. 'She said that I couldn't expect much from you after having not been in contact for so long.'

Sofia's expression soured. That was more like it.

'Of course she did,' Sofia said shaking her head.

'No, you misunderstood . . . '

Sofia looked up sharply and Jack winced.

'I just meant that Annabel was taking your side.'

Sofia doubted that very much and took a sip of coffee to try to hide her expression.

'She said she thought I had behaved terribly and I couldn't just come crashing back into your life. She said it wasn't fair.'

Sofia frowned again as she found herself agreeing with Annabel for the first time, ever. Then a thought struck her.

'Perhaps Annabel was interested in you herself, have you considered that?'

'Sofia, Annabel is not interested in me, that much I can tell you.' He tilted his head to one side. 'Are you jealous?'

Sofia saw amusement dance in his eyes and it was so like the look Annabel would wear when she had scored a point over Sofia, that she had to look away.

'It is nothing to do with me what you do with your life, Jack. Not any more. You made that much abundantly clear at the time.'

'Like I said, I was a fool.'

Sofia nodded. That much she could agree with him on.

'So, we have agreed that you were an

idiot but why are you here?'

Jack reached across the small table and took her hand in his. Sofia felt her breath catch in her throat.

'I'm here to beg your forgiveness and to ask you to take me back.'

Broken Dreams

Sofia stared at him. She wondered if she was still asleep, if the day had not yet started. Perhaps the part of her mind, where she kept all her memories of Jack, had somehow been let free in her dreams.

She almost jumped in surprise when she felt his hand squeeze hers. It felt real. She could hear the noise of the city as a backdrop and smell the heady scent of coffee wafting out of the café.

None of her dreams of this moment had felt this real.

She had dreamed often of Jack appearing out of the blue and begging her to take him back. In her dreams she had laughed and cried and fallen into his arms but this, it seemed, was not a dream.

'Sofia?' Jack's voice broke through her daydreams.

Sofia looked at him. She couldn't think what to say. She had spent too many nights dreaming that this would happen and now it was. Now, she wasn't sure what she wanted.

'I know this must seem like it came out of the blue. Annabel told me that it wasn't a smart move not to be in contact for all that time but I wanted to be sure that I had everything in place.'

Sofia shook her head. She couldn't begin to imagine what Jack felt he needed in place, before he simply picked up the phone.

All of that pain and heartache that she had been going through and he could have eased it by a simple phone call and yet he chose not to.

'Do you have any idea what the last eight months have been like for me?' Sofia's voice cracked on the words. She looked up at him and saw pain on his face but it didn't make her feel any better.

'I'm sorry, Sofia, I thought . . . '

'Did you think?' Sofia broke in. 'Did

198

you think about me at all?'

'Of course, every day. I know I've been a fool but Sofia, please . . . '

'Or were you just thinking about yourself?'

That brought Jack up short. He sat upright.

'What do you mean?'

'We had our whole life planned out together and then without warning you announced that you had changed your mind. You just walked away and left me.

'For eight months I had no idea how you were or what you thought or felt.

'You left me alone to try and put the pieces of my life back together, which I did, with the help of my friends and family.'

Sofia moved her chair back so that she could release her hand from his grip.

'It may have seemed like a good plan to you but for me . . . it just seems cruel and then when I finally feel my life is getting back on an even keel you turn up, out of the blue and announce that you think you've changed your mind.'

'Sofia, I'm sorry, I thought that I needed to . . . '

'What you needed to do was not ignore me for eight months. I can't do this.' Sofia stood up. All she wanted was to get away. The dream that she had had for all those months now seemed to feel like a nightmare.

'Sofia, I love you.'

His words were enough to still her escape for a few moments.

'I love you, too, I probably always will — but I'm not sure that is enough any more. What is it that you want from me?'

'I just want the chance to prove to you that I made a terrible mistake, that we could be happy again.'

'And you thought that you could do all that in two weeks? Did you think that you would appear and I would throw everything away that I've worked so hard for, turn my back on my family, who were there for me and just get on the next plane back to the UK with you?'

Jack opened his mouth to speak but Sofia waved his words away.

'I might have, if you had turned up a few months ago,' Sofia continued. 'I was so sad and I missed you so badly but now — now I wonder if I know you at all. I feel like a favourite toy that you grew out of but now suddenly want back, at least for a time. Well, I can't go through that again.'

Sofia turned on her heel and walked away. Jack could pay for their coffees, it was the least he could do.

She knew that Maria would be proud of her, was even sure that she had done the right thing, but it didn't help her heart, which felt like it was breaking all over again.

★ ★ ★

Sofia made herself focus on work and pushed away all thoughts of Jack. She would think about it later, when she was at home, when Maria was around and they could talk it all through.

She was sure that Maria would help her make sense of it all.

The guests had all appeared on time, apart from Jack, of course, at the Sagrada Familia and she walked them back to the hotel. Once she had explained the plans for the next day, she left them to their dinners at the hotel and made her way to her own home.

'Sofia, how did it go? Your text message did not give much away.'

Sofia plonked herself down on the sofa and burst into tears. Maria stopped preparing dinner and rushed over, drawing her cousin into her arms, as she had done many times before.

Maria said nothing, just let Sofia cry. When her sobs subsided, Maria handed her some tissues.

'Well that explains the text,' Maria said kindly, squeezing her cousin's hand. 'Do you want to talk about it or would you rather we find something to distract you?'

Sofia managed a watery smile. She knew that her cousin was desperate to know what had happened, but she also knew that she cared for Sofia too much to push her on the matter, if she wasn't ready.

'I'm so confused, Maria. I think I need to talk about it.'

'Good,' Maria said. 'Come into the kitchen and I will cook and you will talk. We cannot let this man ruin our dinner.'

★ ★ ★

Sofia talked, all through the preparation and all through dinner. And by the time they were tucking into the Spanish flan that Maria had made, she was finally done.

'You think he really expects you to go home with him?'

'Yes!' Sofia said indignantly.

'Do you want to?' Maria asked softly.

'No, Maria, of course not, my life is here now. No man is going to make me turn my back on my family or my commitments — especially one who has treated me so badly.'

'I would understand,' Maria said but her eyes were bright. Sofia reached out and pulled her into a one-armed hug.

'If anything, Jack has made me realise even more that this is my home. I'm happy here, Maria. I love my job. Love my life. This is where I want to be.'

'But you must miss home.'

'Sometimes, but my friends are all planning to come out and visit and Mum and Dad are looking to buy a holiday home out here now they are retiring. My life is here, Maria. This is where I want to be.'

'I am glad. I would be very sad to see you go.'

'All I need to do now is survive the next week,' Sofia said ruefully.

'It sounds as if you made your feelings clear?' Maria said, pouring them each a coffee.

'I did, but I doubt Jack will give up so easily. If he is to be believed, he has spent eight months planning this.' Sofia frowned again at the thought. It seemed like such an odd way to go about things and not like Jack at all.

He had said that Annabel had advised against his plan but Sofia was still struggling to believe that she had changed so much since their days at university.

Annabel keeping Jack from her for all this time seemed exactly the sort of thing that she would advise.

Perhaps she was hoping that when Jack came home, heartbroken, that she would be there to comfort him and then they might progress from just being friends.

'I can see your mind whirring, Sofia. I hope you have not changed your mind?'

'No,' Sofia said, 'just thinking about whether Annabel is behind everything that happened.'

'Perhaps . . . but the best thing you can do is not spend any more of your time thinking of her. If she is the person that you say she is, that is exactly what she wants.'

Bolt from the Blue

Sofia walked into the hotel thinking about the tour that had been arranged for that day. She would be taking the group to Park Guell, another of her favourite places. She had arranged for an early breakfast — there was little shade at the park and they would be most comfortable touring in the morning.

Jack, for a change, was one of the first to arrive, accompanying Tony and Greta. Tony was sitting in the wheelchair and Jack was pushing him.

'Good morning,' Sofia greeted them. 'I'm glad you have decided to use the wheelchair, Tony. It's a long walk round and I think you would find it hard work on your crutches.

'Jack persuaded me and has offered to be my chauffeur, so to speak.'

'That's very kind of you,' Sofia said

to Jack, hoping that they would be able to get through the day without any reference to their discussion the day before.

'No problem at all. I was wondering if I could have a quick word with you?' Jack asked and Sofia forced down a sigh.

Greta and Tony were looking up expectantly and Sofia felt that the only way to avoid a scene was to do what Jack asked.

'Of course. We have a few moments before Tino will be here to collect us.'

Sofia looked at her watch. It was more like 10 minutes but all she could do was hope that Tino would come early and cut the conversation short.

She tried to remember what a tour was like without all the added drama but tours like that seemed to have happened a lifetime ago.

Jack stepped away from the Whiteheads and Sofia followed him to a quiet corner of the wide reception area. Sofia hoped that they were not be overheard.

'About yesterday . . . ' Jack started to say.

'I'm glad we talked, Jack,' Sofia rushed in, 'but I hope you understand how I feel. This is my home, Jack, and I won't be coming back to the UK with you.'

'I didn't actually ask you to,' Jack said, raising an eyebrow, and Sofia could feel her cheeks flush with embarrassment. It wasn't possible that she had misunderstood him, surely?

He had made his thoughts quite plain. She closed her eyes briefly and wished that the conversation had gone the way she had practised in her head all night.

'Then I suppose I must have misunderstood you again.' Her eyes challenged him to lay the blame at her feet but he just smiled.

'I think it was more to do with the fact that you didn't let me finish.'

'I thought I had heard enough,' Sofia said a little more defensively than she had planned.

'I know that I upset you and I'm

sorry. Please believe me, that was not my intention. I should have explained more about my plan.'

Sofia nodded but she wasn't sure that she wanted to hear any more.

'I should have led with what I was doing yesterday morning but I thought you were owed an explanation first.'

Sofia now looked and felt bewildered.

'Jack, you are making even less sense than yesterday,' she finally said when he appeared lost in thought.

'You're right and we don't really have the time so I will get to the point. Yesterday I went for a job interview.'

Sofia's eyes went wide.

'I didn't want to tell you because I wasn't sure if I would get it but they told me at the interview that I had and well . . . now I'm telling you.'

He looked so pleased with himself that Sofia was momentarily speechless. It must have been a telephone interview.

'Congratulations,' she said mechanically, 'but I'm not sure what that has to do with our situation.'

'It has everything to do with it, since the job is based here in Barcelona.'

Sofia was sure she had misheard, or perhaps she was trapped in another dream. Had Jack just said what she thought he had?

'What?' she squeaked. 'What do you mean?'

'I have a job here, in Barcelona.'

Sofia stared.

'But you don't speak Spanish.' Sofia knew that probably wasn't the most important point but that was all she could come up with from her stunned brain.

'I do now,' Jack said, looking very impressed with himself. Sofia blinked.

'Since when?'

'Since I started learning it when I heard you had come to Spain.'

'And you now speak it well enough to get a job here?'

'I know you find it hard to believe but yes, I do.' He sounded a little hurt at the suggestion that he might not yet be ready to speak Spanish at work.

'But you're a paramedic. Please tell me you haven't given that up?' Sofia couldn't believe what was happening.

Jack had wanted to be a paramedic since he was a small boy and she couldn't bear the thought that he might be giving that up, giving up everything for her.

'And I will be a paramedic again. I have a job as an ambulance technician. When I have completed my first year and if I make the grade, they will sponsor me to do the conversion course.'

Sofia gasped. She couldn't believe this was happening. In fact, she could feel the air rushing in her ears and for a moment she thought she was going to faint.

'OK, you need to sit down,' Jack said calmly. In full paramedic mode he steered her to the nearest chair and sat her down. 'Take some slow deep breaths.'

Sofia did as she was told and the rushing air stopped and the black dots disappeared from in front of her eyes.

'I know that in fairy tales the prince likes it when the princess swoons but in reality, it tends to end in head injuries and trips to the local hospital.'

Sofia looked up at him.

He smiled.

'I know it's a lot to take in.'

Sofia nodded her head at that massive understatement.

'And by the looks of things you are going to need a bit of time before you are ready to talk about this again. So, I'll leave you to compose yourself and go and help Tony to get on to the coach.'

Sofia looked out of the large windows at the front of the hotel and could see that Tino had arrived.

She wasn't sure that her legs were ready to take her weight and so she just sat there and watched Jack wheel Tony out to the coach, flashing a smile in her direction as he passed.

Sofia did her best to focus on the tour. She had so many facts and figures about the park, its gardens and architecture, not to mention Antoni Gaudi, the designer behind the splendour, but it wasn't easy.

Jack stayed with Tony and Greta as he had promised and, other than listening attentively when Sofia spoke, kept out of her way.

Sofia felt like she was the one who needed a holiday.

Of all the scenarios she had considered, Jack moving to Spain was not one of them. Now he had announced what he was doing, she didn't know how she felt.

The tour seemed to drag when usually it seemed to whizz by and she was relieved when they finally got back to the hotel.

A Problem Shared . . .

With the guests settled and happy, Sofia was planning to head back to her apartment with her laptop. It seemed safer than staying at the hotel where she might bump into Jack.

She had reached the doors when she heard someone calling her name. For a brief second, she thought about pretending she hadn't heard but her conscience wouldn't let her. She turned around, one hand on the door to give the impression that she was in a hurry and came to face with Barbs Turner.

'Hello, Mrs Turner. What can I do for you?'

'I just wanted to see how you were. You seemed a little distracted through the tour today and I wondered if everything was all right?'

Sofia felt heat rise in her cheeks but made herself smile.

'I'm fine, thank you for asking. I'm sorry if I seemed a little distracted. I had some news that was on my mind today and I'm afraid it may have put me off my game a little.'

'Oh, dear, well, I hope it wasn't bad news.'

'To be honest, Mrs Turner, I'm not really sure.'

'Perhaps you would like to talk about it?' Mrs Turner smiled at Sofia and in that moment reminded her so much of her mum that she nearly said yes, which would not exactly have been professional.

'Oh, Mrs Turner, you're very kind but I couldn't possibly burden you with this. You are on holiday, after all.'

Sofia felt Mrs Turner's assessing eyes.

'Sofia, Mr Turner and I raised five daughters, three of whom are married. I hope you won't mind me guessing that young Jack has something to do with your, er, discombobulation?'

Sofia smiled — she couldn't help it.

'Trust me, my dear, I've seen all my girls through every type of romantic situation and I would love to help if I can.

'But please don't feel under any pressure. I appreciate that I am a stranger and one of my daughters, Grace, would be most displeased with me right now for, as she would stay, sticking my nose in.'

'Not at all,' Sofia said. 'To be honest, it might help if I could just say what I'm thinking out loud.'

'Well, that's settled, then. I am an excellent listener. I've had to be with that many girls in the house.

'Why don't we step out and find somewhere quiet, and you can tell me all about it.'

Sofia took Mrs Turner to one of her favourite cafés. It was down a back street and had tables set out on the pavement. The road was quiet and so, for the city, it was remarkably peaceful.

Mrs Turner had been true to her word and had listened, without making comment, to everything that Sofia had to say.

It had all come out as a jumble, so many different thoughts and feelings, but Mrs Turner seemed to take this in her stride. Apparently raising five girls really did prepare you for anything.

'Oh, dear, it really does make one wonder sometimes,' Mrs Turner said when it was clear that Sofia had said all she was going to for the moment.

'I know I ought to be grateful that Jack has . . . '

Mrs Turner gave Sofia a look and she stopped talking.

'Oh, no, my dear, certainly not! My comment was directed firmly at Jack and men in general. I wonder where they get their ideas from and how they manage to get it so wrong. I'm not surprised that you're feeling confused.'

'Thank you.'

Mrs Turner raised a questioning eyebrow and Sofia smiled.

'It's nice to know that someone else understands how I feel. I was beginning to wonder if it was just me.'

'No woman likes to be ignored for

months and then presented with a fait accompli.'

The waiter appeared and Sofia requested another pot of tea for them both. One of the other things she liked about this café was that they served proper English tea.

'I must say I am surprised at Jack,' Mrs Turner said. 'He seems like such a sensible chap and what with him being a paramedic . . . well. Not that any of that matters now. What matters is what you want to do next.'

'That's just it. I have no idea. I feel as if I have been . . . ' Sofia searched for the right words.

'Ambushed?' Mrs Turner offered and Sofia nodded vigorously — that was exactly it. She felt like she had been blind-sided and not just with this latest announcement, with pretty much every-thing that had happened since Jack stepped off the plane.

'Perhaps you should tell him that?' Mrs Turner said, pouring tea for both of them.

'But he has given up so much for me ... Don't you think that would be a little churlish?'

'Not at all,' Mrs Turner said sternly. 'The man deserted you, left you to your broken heart and then just decided to reappear in your life months later, without so much as a note, or should I say, text? I suppose that is more the thing these days?'

Sofia giggled. Already she felt so much better.

'If you would like my advice ... ' Mrs Turner paused until Sofia nodded that she would. 'Then I think you should tell him honestly how you feel.'

Sofia winced at the thought.

'It might help to practise. What would you like to say to him?'

Sofia thought about this and took a sip of tea. Perhaps it wasn't that she didn't know what to say, maybe it was more that she wasn't sure how to say it. She sighed.

Mrs Turner patted her hand in understanding.

'Why don't we start with the basics? Do you still love him?'

Sofia nodded, feeling shy all of a sudden.

'I think I do but so much has changed. I'm not sure it is the same love any more.'

'Then I think you should tell him that.'

'I don't want to hurt him.'

'I know, my dear, but pretending your feelings are anything but what you have just told me will hurt him worse in the long run.'

'But he has given up so much.'

'That was entirely his decision. Perhaps he understands how you feel and wants to ensure that you both have the opportunity to spend time together to see if you do still feel the same?'

Sofia blinked. She had never thought of it like that.

'Do you think so?'

'He may have gone about things all the wrong way but I do believe that he loves you and that he's sorry for making such a mess of things.

'But that is not the point. Right now, you need to think about how *you* feel and what it is that you need from him. His feelings do not override your own.'

'I need time,' Sofia said. 'I need time to think about everything. And I think we need to take it slowly and see how things go before we make any serious decisions.'

'Then that's what you tell him,' Mrs Turner said as if it were all agreed, 'and I would speak to him soon. These things only get harder if you wait.'

'Thank you for listening, Mrs Turner. I feel bad for taking you away from your holiday.'

'Nonsense. I'm more than happy to help and all of us like to feel useful from time to time.'

'Well, you've been wonderful. I wish there was something I could do for you.'

'This tour has been wonderful, Sofia. It has been everything I imagined it would be and that is down to you. So I think we can call it even.' Mrs Turner smiled as she stood up.

'Now I'm going to head back to the hotel. I am meeting the Whitehouses for dinner and I don't want to be late.'

'Let me walk you back,' Sofia offered.

'No need, dear. I am quite capable of finding my own way. I suggest you go home and get a good night's sleep. You need to be rested if you are going to speak to Jack in the morning.'

Let Bygones Be Bygones

Sofia arrived at the hotel after a good night's sleep, which was surprising considering all that she had ahead of her that day.

When she had arrived home, she had told Maria everything that had happened and all the advice Mrs Turner had given. To her surprise, Maria and Mrs Turner were in agreement.

Sofia needed to tell Jack exactly how she felt and that was what she was going to do. It was a relief to have finally decided on something; and all she needed to do now was to act on her decision.

Sofia waited outside the dining-room. Her plan was to ask Jack to have breakfast with her, alone. She was no longer worried what the guests thought, since she was certain there would be no scene today — just two old friends having a conversation.

Most of the guests had arrived and taken their seats when Jack finally appeared. His face lit up when he saw her and Sofia bit back a smile. She needed to be honest with him and not won over by one simple expression.

'Good morning, Jack. I was wondering if you would like to have breakfast with me.'

'That would be lovely. Would you mind if a friend joined us?'

Sofia stared. Of course she minded. She needed to speak to Jack alone. As fond as she was of the other guests, she was hoping that just this once she would be able to have some time alone with Jack.

Sofia realised that she hadn't seen Mrs Turner yet and so was sure that when she arrived, she would take the hint very quickly and head off to have breakfast with some of the other guests.

The lift opened and Sofia looked up expectantly. Mrs Turner stepped out and waved to Sofia, who waved back.

Mrs Turner didn't walk straight towards them, but waited until another figure stepped out of the lift.

Sofia's eyes widened. The last person she had expected, after Jack, was also here in Spain. Mrs Turner and Annabel chatted as they walked over.

'Morning, Sofia,' Mrs Turner said, 'I've just bumped into Annabel, a friend of yours who has come over on a surprise visit!' Mrs Turner was smiling so broadly that Sofia forced her face into a sort of half smile and hoped her real thoughts were hidden by the look of shock, which could have been surprise.

Sofia had mentioned Annabel in passing to Mrs Turner, when they had talked the day before but had not gone into any of the details.

'Annabel. I never expected to see you here,' Sofia said with forced gaiety.

'Well, I'll leave you young people to catch up,' Mrs Turner said as she sailed past.

Having only moments ago hoped that

Mrs Turner would read the situation and absent herself so that Sofia could speak to Jack, all Sofia wanted her to do now was stay and have breakfast with them.

'I thought I'd pop over for a few days,' Annabel said with a smile and Sofia could detect none of the usual hidden dig or meaning. 'Jack said I should come over and speak to you myself.'

Sofia felt all wrong-footed.

'Really? Well, why don't we go and get some breakfast and then we can . . . catch up?' She led the way into the dining-room before any more could be said.

Once they were settled at the table and the waiter had taken their order, there were no longer any excuses. Jack was looking between the two women and looking mildly amused.

'OK, ladies . . . normally it's me that doesn't know what to say.'

Both Sofia and Annabel raised an eyebrow at that, as nothing was further from the truth.

'Annabel, since you've travelled all this way, why don't you go first?' Jack suggested.

Sofia looked at Jack. It wasn't as if she had much of anything to say to Annabel. What did you say to the person who had seemed to take an instant dislike to you and had made that fact clear to everyone else on your course at university?

Annabel hadn't exactly made Sofia's life miserable but she certainly hadn't made it any happier for her.

Annabel was twisting her napkin in her lap and Sofia had never seen her like this. Jack put a hand on her arm and Annabel looked up.

They exchanged a silent message and Annabel took a deep breath.

Sofia felt a flash of jealousy at the ease at which they could communicate without words and once again her mind raced with what might Annabel's true motives.

'I wanted to say,' Annabel said slowly as if she were carefully picking her words, 'that I was sorry for the way I treated you at university.' Some of the tension seemed to leave Annabel and she looked more relaxed.

'OK . . . ' Sofia said, still feeling a little confused. Why this and why now?

'I've felt bad about the whole situation since we graduated but we lost touch,' Annabel continued.

Sofia personally thought that they had never been in touch and so simply nodded.

'You see, I was pretty unhappy at university. I was missing home but didn't think I could tell anyone. I thought they would think I was immature.' Annabel looked up and Sofia blinked in surprise.

Annabel was the last person she would have imagined as homesick but perhaps that was the point.

'You seemed so at ease, so unfazed by it all and then you met Jack and you were the perfect couple. I was horribly jealous of you, Sofia, and so I lashed out.

'I suppose deep down I wanted you

to feel some of what I was feeling. It was incredibly childish of me and I am so, so sorry.'

Sofia stared at Annabel but could detect nothing other than honesty in her open face.

'I had no idea,' Sofia said, shaking her head at the revelation.

If she had been asked to guess, and she had tried herself for almost three years, she would never have come up with that as an explanation of Annabel's behaviour.

'It's not an excuse,' Annabel added hurriedly, 'but I felt I owed you an explanation as well as an apology.'

Sofia took a few moments to digest all this new information as the waiter appeared with their plates of food.

'Thank you,' Sofia said and found that she meant it. 'I have to admit I was confused as to what I had done to make you dislike me.'

'It's embarrassing to even think about. I was so unkind to you.'

Sofia made a decision in that moment.

There had been times in her life when she hadn't behaved as she knew she ought and Annabel had taken a brave, not to mention expensive step, to come all the way out to Spain to apologise.

'Please don't be embarrassed. I'm glad that you've told me what it was all about. Perhaps we can both let go of the past?' Sofia smiled at Annabel and for the first time ever was offered a smile in reply.

'I'd like that,' Annabel said as Jack clapped his hands together, looking thoroughly pleased with himself.

'Am I to take it that you had something to do with this?' Sofia asked.

Jack shrugged.

'When I met up with Annabel again and she told me how she felt about it all, well, I knew that it was unfinished business for you, too.

'So I thought it would be good to get you both together so you could sort it out.'

'How did you meet up?' Sofia asked.

'My little boy fell over and banged his

head. Jack was one of the paramedics who responded,' Annabel said, smiling at Jack. 'I was in a right state and he calmed me down until Toby came home from work.'

'Toby?' Sofia asked.

'My husband.' Annabel's eyes lit up. 'We've been married for nearly four years.'

'And was your little boy all right?'

'He's fine. Just a little glue to stick his head back together.' Annabel gave a rueful smile. 'Toby and Jack hit it off, since they're both big rugby fans, and so I asked Jack round for dinner to say thank you for all his help.'

Sofia nodded slowly as her concerns and worries slowly dissolved. Never in a million years could she have imagined that this was how this would turn out.

'Annabel asked me how you were. She assumed that we were still together,' Jack added a little wistfully.

'When Jack told me what he had done, I couldn't believe it — and I told him so.'

'In no uncertain terms,' Jack added, smiling.

'And that's when I knew what I needed to do. I thought it might go some way to make up for how I behaved.' Annabel looked sad again and Sofia reached across and squeezed her hand. Sofia felt like a weight had lifted, one that she hadn't even realised was still there.

'So Annabel taught me Spanish,' Jack announced as the last piece of the puzzle for Sofia dropped into place.

'I should say at this point I called him all kinds of idiot for not getting in touch with you sooner.

'But he was so set on his plan that I couldn't persuade him otherwise.'

Sofia raised an eyebrow at Jack, who looked sheepish.

'Yes, I think we have established that Annabel was right and I was wrong.'

Annabel laughed and shook her head.

'Well, since I expect you need to have a conversation that would be easier if I wasn't present. I'm going to head up to

my room and get my swimming cos-
tume. I feel the pool is calling me,'
Annabel said.

'You would be welcome to come on
the tour today, if you like.'

Annabel looked genuinely surprised
and pleased.

'Thanks for the offer but to be
honest, with a two-year-old at home, I
never have the opportunity to just sit
and read a magazine. I promised myself
I could, if we could sort things out
between us.'

Sofia smiled.

'Of course. Well, you go and enjoy
yourself. We'll be back for dinner, if
you'd like to join us.'

'I'd love to,' Annabel said with a
broad grin before she headed back to
the lift and up to her room.

'I think you looked more surprised
to see Annabel than you did me,' Jack
said. Sofia turned her attention back to
him.

'Not even close,' Sofia said and Jack
grinned ruefully.

'When you asked me to breakfast I wondered if you had something you want to talk to me about?' Jack looked hopeful and Sofia could see the man that she known so well sitting beside her, for the first time since he had arrived . . .

'Actually, I do.' Sofia said, taking a deep breath and trying to remember all the advice that Mrs Turner and Maria had given her.

Falling in Love Again

'You arriving out of the blue was a surprise,' Sofia began.

'I think we've established that I was a bit of an idiot for that,' Jack said and he looked slightly worried but was doing his best to hide it.

'A lot has changed since we were together.'

It was a statement more than a question but Jack nodded his head.

'And I think we both need time to get to know each other again,' Sofia said, finding the words surprisingly hard to say.

'When you first arrived, I assumed that you thought I would drop everything and just come back to the UK with you.'

Jack opened his mouth to speak but Sofia held up a hand.

'I now know that your plan was

different. So am I right to assume that we are both on the same page?'

Jack raised an eyebrow, as if asking if he could speak. Sofia rolled her eyes and waved a hand, to indicate, yes, he could speak now.

'That was my plan. I feel the same. I love you, Sofia, that hasn't changed and never will, whatever you decide, but I remember you talking about living in Spain and when I heard that you had come over here, I knew that I couldn't just expect you to come back to the UK to see if we could make a go of it again.

'I knew that we needed time and that if Spain was where you wanted to be then I would need to get my life to a point where I could live here happily, too.'

'But you're giving up so much,' Sofia said, voicing one of her concerns.

'Am I? For sunshine, a beautiful city and you?'

'You know what I mean. You're leaving behind all your friends and family.'

'We aren't on the moon, Sofia. They can come and visit and I plan to go home and see them, too.'

'I suppose what I'm asking is, are you sure?'

'I don't think either of us is a hundred per cent sure, but that's kind of the point. We need to start afresh and see if we can make things work between us. Don't you think?'

Sofia nodded. She wasn't sure that she would be able to find the words to say anything in that moment.

She couldn't really imagine how all of this could have worked out any more perfectly. Jack had given her the gift of time. There would be no pressure now.

He wasn't asking her to choose between the commitment she had made to Maria and her uncle and him.

And who knew? Perhaps they could have a whole new life together here in Spain.

'So we're agreed?' Jack asked and tentatively reached a hand out for hers. Sofia smiled.

'Yes, I'd like to get to know you again, Jack.'

'Good. Well, I won't be on the tour today as I'm looking for somewhere to live, but I'll make sure that I'm back for dinner with you and Annabel later, if that's all right?'

'That will be perfect,' Sofia said.

'In that case, I should let you go. I think your tour guests are waiting for you.'

Sofia followed Jack's gaze to the guests that were standing together in the reception area but looking through the window of the restaurant and taking in everything that was happening.

Sofia could feel herself blush as they all smiled at her and a few of them clapped and cheered.

She looked at her watch and realised the time. She was late! No wonder they were all standing there staring.

She leaped up from her seat and Jack laughed, it was a wonderful sound, one that she thought she would never get to hear again.

Jack stood up too and walked around the table.

'May I?' he asked with a small, gentlemanly bow. Their eyes locked and Sofia felt as if she had come home.

'You may,' she said softly as Jack helped her to her feet before leaning across and kissing her gently on the lips.

They were rewarded by another, louder round of applause and Jack pulled her into a tight hug.

'I will see you later for dinner, Sofia. Don't fall in love with anyone else while I'm away from you.'

Sofia rolled her eyes.

'As if I would,' she said and then wriggled from his arms and walked towards her waiting guests with her head held high.

Out in the reception area she was greeted by warm hugs and smiles.

Tino had arrived in the coach and one by one the guests climbed on board until it was just Sofia and Mrs Turner left.

'I had a feeling it would all work out,'

Mrs Turner whispered in Sofia's ear.

'Well, your excellent advice certainly helped it to happen,' Sofia said, smiling so widely that her cheeks were starting to hurt.

'I always say to my girls that if it's meant to be, it will work itself out, as long as you keep an open mind.

'Did you tell him everything you had planned to?'

'I did and it seems we're in perfect agreement. We both need time to get to know each other again and see how we feel.'

'And how do you feel?' Mrs Turner said smiling at Sofia.

'Like I might be falling in love all over again.'

'Have a good day, ladies,' Jack said as he walked past, and Sofia wondered how much of the conversation he had overheard.

He reached for both of their hands and kissed them in turn, causing both Sofia and Mrs Turner to giggle like schoolgirls.

Jack held Sofia away from him as if he needed to memorise her face.

'I love you, Sofia Garcia, I know that we said we would take things slowly but I have to tell you that.'

'And I love you, too, Jack. Now go! You are making me late — again.'

Jack looked towards the coach and the faces watching them. He waved and a few people waved back.

'Till tonight,' he said.

'Till tonight,' Sofia said and watched him go before climbing on to the coach and getting back to work.

Sweet Dreams

Sofia's eyes scanned the airport arrivals hall for the faces she was looking for. Then she saw them and waved frantically.

'Over here!' she called as Mrs Turner and the Whitehouses spotted her and headed towards her to exchange smiles, hugs and greetings.

'I'm so glad you could come,' Sofia said, squeezing Mrs Turner tightly.

'We were honoured to be invited,' Tony said.

As they headed to Sofia's car, Mrs Turner slipped her arm though Sofia's.

'How are you feeling?' Mrs Turner asked.

'Excited and a little scared.'

'Exactly how you are supposed to feel,' Mrs Turner said approvingly.

Sofia drove her guests to the hotel on the outskirts of Barcelona and her dad was waiting to help with the luggage.

'Thanks, Dad,' she said, smiling at him. 'Tony, Greta, Barbs, let me introduce my dad, Paulo.' There was shaking of hands and warm greetings. 'And my mum, Isobel.'

Out of the corner of her eye, Sofia saw Jack walking towards her. She smiled up at him as he pulled her into a hug.

'Jack!' Mrs Turner squealed. 'It is so good to see you again.'

'And you, Mrs Turner. Sofia and I were so happy that you were be able to make it.'

'I wouldn't have missed it for the world,' Mrs Turner announced.

'Well, let's get you settled. We have a celebration dinner to get ready for,' Jack said and led the way into the hotel.

Sofia was sure that she wouldn't sleep a wink but she did and as they had been for some time, her dreams were all happy ones.

When Sofia woke in the morning, Maria, her mum and her aunties were all waiting to fuss over her as she got ready.

She wondered what Jack was doing at that moment and the others laughed as she seemed lost in a dreamy romantic haze.

'My darling, you look beautiful,' her dad announced when he was finally allowed into the room.

'You look very handsome,' Sofia said, patting the front of her dad's suit.

'You look like your mother,' he added as he reached out a hand for his wife and pulled her into the three-person embrace.

'Well, I am wearing her dress,' Sofia said as she looked down at the lace covered dress that was absolutely perfect.

'Are you ready?' her dad asked and Sofia nodded. 'And you are sure?'

Sofia looked surprised.

'I'm your dad, I have to ask the important questions.'

'I've never been more sure of anything in my life.'

He leaned down and kissed her on the forehead.

'In that case, we should go. We don't want to keep Jack waiting.'

Outside, Tino was ready, dressed in a smart suit, the car decorated with white roses.

'Miss Sofia, you look magnificent!' Tino beamed as he opened the car door and her father helped her to gather up her dress.

The staff at the hotel had all turned out to wave her off and Sofia felt as if she were the belle in a parade.

Butterflies fluttered in her chest as Tino pulled the car up outside the small church where members of her family had been married for hundreds of years.

Her father held out his hand.

'Jack is a very lucky man,' he said looking at her, 'and I must say I think you have chosen very well.'

'Thank you, Dad. I think I have you

to thank for that. I wanted what you and Mum have.'

He pulled her into a tight hug. The doors to church were opened and Sofia could hear the sound of the organ being played.

'Shall we?' her father said, taking her arm in his.

A year ago, this had all felt like an impossible dream. At the end of the aisle she could see Jack, looking impossibly handsome in his suit, with his brother at his side.

Her father led her down the aisle, before kissing her gently on the cheek and passing her hand from his to Jack's.

Sofia set her eyes on Jack and together they stepped before the priest and made promises to each other before all their family and friends.

When the priest made his final announcement, Jack kissed her and they turned to face the church, which was full to the last seat. Sofia looked out at all the smiling faces. At Annabel and her husband, their little boy standing on the pew so that he could get a better view.

At Mrs Turner and the Whiteheads, beaming up at them and at her parents, arms around each other, with a few happy tears on their cheeks.

Then she looked back to Jack, the man that she had fallen in love with and then fallen in love with all over again.

'Well, Mrs Brown, I think it is time to celebrate,' he said.

'So, do I, Mr Brown, so do I.'

And together, arm in arm, they walked down the aisle to start a new chapter in their life.

We do hope that you have enjoyed reading this large print book.

Did you know that all of our titles are available for purchase?

We publish a wide range of high quality large print books including:
Romances, Mysteries, Classics
General Fiction
Non Fiction and Westerns

Special interest titles available in large print are:
The Little Oxford Dictionary
Music Book, Song Book
Hymn Book, Service Book

Also available from us courtesy of Oxford University Press:
Young Readers' Dictionary
(large print edition)
Young Readers' Thesaurus
(large print edition)

For further information or a free brochure, please contact us at:
Ulverscroft Large Print Books Ltd.,
The Green, Bradgate Road, Anstey,
Leicester, LE7 7FU, England.
Tel: (00 44) **0116 236 4325**
Fax: (00 44) **0116 234 0205**

LEAVING LISA

Angela Britnell

At age seventeen, married with a three-month-old baby and suffering from post-natal depression, all Rosie could see was her life in a cage with a giant lock. Twenty-five years later, after having left her husband Jack and daughter Lisa, she runs her own business in Nashville. But while she's in England, she sees an engagement announcement in the newspaper — Lisa is getting married. And Rosie decides she wants to make contact after all these years, despite fearing their reaction. Will they find room in their hearts for her again?